STARTS WITH A KISS

JANE LYNNE DANIELS

"Jane Lynne's stories are down-to-earth with a touch of whimsy and always entertaining."
—Jami Davenport, award-winning author of *Down by Contact* and *Forward Passes*.

"This novel dazzles."
—Long and Short Romance Reviews on Be *Careful What You Kiss For*

STARTING OVER

Everything will *finally* be better. In college Anya Ramsay made the worst mistake of her life, but a gypsy spell now offers the chance to have done everything different. To have done things right. The college car accident that disfigured her face and paralyzed basketball star Ryder Brandt, the man she's always loved? It'll have never happened. But nothing is ever so easy, just as some things—like Ryder's kiss—can never be forgotten. To rectify all, Anya has to come to terms with who she is and what she's done. Rewriting this mistake will be a ride wilder than the original, but at the end of the trip is a happy ending—and a life with the perfect man for her past, present and future.

STARTS WITH A KISS

JANE LYNNE DANIELS

www.BOROUGHSPUBLISHINGGROUP.com

STARTS WITH A KISS
Copyright © 2015 Dawn Gothro

ISBN 978-1-942886-04-4

To A.G. and S.G., with love and thanks for the encouragement

CONTENTS

STARTS WITH A KISS

PROLOGUE

Sophomore year of college—2005

Anya's nervous laugh caught in her throat as she slipped off the
last bit of her clothing and stood naked in the twilight of the spring
day, the small clearing surrounded by tall trees reaching skyward,
their branches rustling above.

Across from her, Ryder didn't make a sound, instead letting the
smile that stole across his mouth and his sudden intake of breath do
his talking for him.

A flick of his wrist and he was naked now, too, his tall, lean,
and muscled body facing her as they stood at the edge of the gently
gurgling hot springs, barefooted on the stone.

Ryder had been the one to find this place, tucked deep into the
forest. No one else would be there to see or hear them, he'd said.
He'd been right. They were alone.

He put his hand out, tugging on hers, guiding her toward the
water. Anya put one foot in and then the other, as Ryder did the
same. The water was hot, mesmerizing, welcoming.

Together they knelt in the shallow pool, submerging their bodies
up to their necks. The ends of her hair floated behind and then stuck
to her back when she bobbed upward to wrap her arms around
Ryder's back, pressing her body to his.

His groan rumbled through her as he pulled her to him. He
moved back until they lay lengthwise across the pool, the water
acting like a drug that both soothed and excited.

She held him close, so close, reveling in the feel of him, the life
that surged through him and into her, at once protecting and
exposing her. They moved as one, loved as one, and held nothing
back. The realization pierced her soul and heart until she was
vulnerable in places she'd never thought she could be and tender in
places she didn't know she had.

Afterward, she lay with her head against the smooth stone and
looked up to the opening in the night sky framed by the tops of trees
that had witnessed the fierce, gentle urgency of their lovemaking.
Stars twinkled. A soft breeze ruffled the water.

Anya ducked her head below and came back up through the
steam with a smile so big that it felt as though it consumed her entire

body. She reached for Ryder's strong arms and they wrapped around her, holding her tight. He whispered in her ear, his damp cheek against hers, the sensation of his rough whiskers against her skin exhilarating. Then his mouth was on hers and she was again lost, sinking into the essence of him.

That night she knew, with unshakable certainty, she was utterly, hopelessly in love with Ryder Brandt.

And, because of it, she would never be the same again.

CHAPTER ONE

Ten years later

Anya took a bite of the moist wedding cake with lighter-than-air frosting, let it linger on her tongue, and swallowed a mouthful of her own bitterness. She set her fork on the china plate, tipped her head to one side, and pasted a smile on her face, ignoring the roiling in her stomach.

She was happy for her cousin Chase and his bride Emma. Really, she was. They were so in love, their shared bliss practically threw up all over their guests.

Wow. All things considered, she'd been a remarkably bad choice for wedding guest/family representative. Resolved to do better, Anya folded the napkin on her lap and laid it next to her plate. Maybe no one had noticed the vinegar puckering her smile.

In the early evening shadows of the late-spring day, hundreds of white lights shone down on the outdoor stage and dance floor Chase had built. The tables overflowed with food and flowers, and the chairs and tables surrounding the dance floor were covered in white and accented with satin bows, from which dangled silver cowboy boots that looked like oversized charms. The setting was romantic, pristine, and sophisticated country.

Emma glowed in her strapless ivory gown, and Chase looked more handsome in his tux than Anya had ever seen him. Married life already agreed with him and it had been less than an hour since the ceremony.

In a few minutes, country star Lacey Simpson would perform the song Chase and Emma had written together and Lacey had recorded. In a very short time, it had already reached number two on the charts.

The new Mr. and Mrs. Chapman had a perfect life. Anya was glad for them. If it weren't for the hole that other people's joy tore in her heart, she'd be great. Really.

She took a long sip of champagne. The good stuff. Quality alcohol might be just the thing to penetrate the petulance curled up inside her throat.

"It is you I have come to see," announced a voice from a chair close by.

Anya turned to see an older woman with orange hair, paper-white skin, and bright pink lipstick. She wore a dark purple dress and a jumble of metal bangles on both wrists.

"Are you talking to me?" Perfect. Now she was doing a bad Robert De Niro, on top of everything else. This day just could not get any better. "I mean, hello." She re-pasted her polite guest smile on her face. If she could *keep* it on, no one would ever have to know how bitter she'd become at the age of thirty. Just wait until she turned fifty. She'd be an evil cackler like the Wicked Witch of the West, with a face to match. Minus the flying monkeys to do her every bidding.

"Yes. You." The woman straightened and her bangles clanked together. "Hello."

Anya took in the riot of color and odd accent that was this unusual woman, and dipped her chin, letting her hair swing forward. "I don't believe we've met," she said.

The woman made a *pffft* sound. "Of course not. Did I say this?"

Oh. "I'm Anya Ramsey. Chase's cousin."

The woman nodded. "And I am Madame Claire," she said.

R-i-g-h-t. "Very nice to meet you, Madame, um, Claire. But I think you're mistaking me for someone else."

The woman raised long fingers thick with rings, flicking the comment way as if it were a pesky fly. "I am never mistaken. Even when I do not ask for this, it comes."

Anya wondered if a local mental health facility could be missing a patient. She dropped her voice, hoping it sounded calming. "Did you see? Lacey Simpson is getting ready to sing."

"This does not matter."

"She's very good. We don't want to miss her." Anya began to sidle one foot away.

"I am not here for this Lacey Simpson."

Anya stilled her foot. She sighed. Much as she would like to, she couldn't leave. This woman might need help. She must have snuck in when the security guards weren't looking. Madame Claire would be hard to miss, but it could have happened. "You *are* here for the wedding?"

"Of course I am here for the wedding." An offended sniff. "It is because of me, is it not, that there *is* a wedding."

Interesting. "So you've known Chase and Emma for…a while?"

"This I did not say."

"Oh." All things considered, the woman wasn't saying much of anything. Anya would have to get someone over here to help. Discreetly. She began scanning the crowd.

Bony fingers grasped her arm. Startled, Anya looked down to see white lights glinting off manicured nails. "What I have to say to you, it is important."

"Um, okay." Anya wondered if she could signal one of the security guards without causing a commotion. "Go ahead. I'm listening." She wasn't, she was trying to get help, but the woman didn't have to know that.

"No. You must meet me tomorrow," Madame Claire said. "Here, right now, this is not so good for talking."

Ummmm, *no*. "Thanks. So much," Anya said, "but—"

"Tomorrow."

"I'm not in town for long. Maybe next time?" She glanced down and scooted her chair a few inches away, trying to make it look as though it were something to do with the ground instead of the strange person who had Anya locked in her grasp. Footsteps on the stage caused her to look up again. "Oh, it's Lacey—"

Instead of releasing her, the fingers pressed harder into her arm. Madame Claire leaned toward Anya's ear. "Your biggest regret in life. It has to do with the accident, does it not?"

Anya froze. The accident.

"Yes, I see now," the woman continued. "You were the one to cause this accident. Driving. And there was a man with you. His injuries, they were—"

Anya felt her cheeks flame. "Stop!" she bit out, surprising even herself with the force of her delivery. She sucked in a breath. "Please. Stop talking." Ryder's face flashed before her mind's eye. Her best friend, the love of her life. Dynamic, gorgeous, smart. A star university basketball player on a full-ride scholarship. Likely headed for the NBA. Everyone had said so.

Until the night Anya had made a critical mistake driving, smashing Ryder's car into another vehicle with a sickening crunch of metal and shattered glass.

"This scar on your face," Madame Claire observed. "You wear it like a, what is it called? A medal? No, a badge."

Of shame. A four-inch badge of shame. Under her left cheekbone, where everyone could see it. Anya's breath came faster and her heart pounded violently. This woman had no right to bring up the accident. She gripped the edges of her chair with both hands and made a conspicuous shift to the right. Madame Claire's hand fell away and Anya ducked her chin so her hair would completely cover her face.

"It does not have to be so. I can erase the mistake from this life of yours. Poof! It will never have happened."

It will never have happened. As the woman's words sank in, two distinct emotions—fury and hope—lined up inside Anya and squared off, ready to fight it out. Anya turned to her left to hiss from under the cover of her hair, "You shouldn't say things like that, things that aren't possible."

"Possible for you to do, no. For me, yes. One time only."

One time only. Fury shoved hope aside, dropped to its knee, and fired off a round. "This isn't funny," Anya said, "and I don't think my cousin and his wife would appreciate you trying to sell me something, some buy-now-get-two-free, at their wedding reception."

"Is not true."

She's crazy. Be nice. Under the cover of Chase's father introducing a beaming Lacey Simpson, Anya struggled to replace the version of herself that fired at intruders with a more polite edition. Before she could get there, the woman spoke again.

"You will come to see me. Tomorrow morning, nine o'clock. At that restaurant in town, the one with the blueberry pancakes. We will talk, you and I."

Poof! It will never have happened. Anya blinked hard to hold back unwanted and unexpected tears, lifting her chin to focus on the stage. Lacey Simpson thanked Chase's father for the introduction and picked up the microphone. The band struck up the first notes of the hit Chase and Emma had cowritten, *Heart Pine Beams.*

Anya had been doing so well playing the nice wedding guest, she thought to herself. Up until Madame Claire's arrival. "Go away," Anya whispered to the woman. "Please. Just go away." As always happened when someone drew attention to her scar, it began to feel like a neon blinking light.

Most of the time, she could keep it from drawing too much attention. Or at least keep people from pointing it out. This woman had practically dragged a giant magnifying glass over to prop it up against Anya's face.

"My feet, they are tired. I will leave now." Madame Claire's sigh was audible despite Lacey's singing and the guests' roars of appreciation. "We will meet tomorrow."

"Thank you, but *no*."

She felt the other woman stand, the slight ripple of air as Madame Claire again leaned close to her ear. "You want to live with this scar in your heart and on your face, this is fine. You do not, you come to talk to me. And if you do not believe what I say is so, all you must do is look at the bride."

The sharp answer that had sprung to Anya's lips died on them just as quickly. "Emma?"

"Emma," the woman said, pronouncing the name like *Eeema*. "One regret she had. Now she has none. Poof."

Anya blinked, trying to take this in. She began to sputter another question, but when she turned, she saw that Madame Claire had left. The orange hair bobbed above the assembled guests and then disappeared behind them, back toward the field where cars were parked in orderly rows.

For a moment, Anya thought about going after her. But instead, she sank lower into her chair, pulled her hair over her cheek, and pondered the woman's comment all through Lacey Simpson's brief set.

Erase a mistake. *Right.* A responsible, decent, normal person wouldn't throw something like that out there, whisper it to the universe for people to irrationally hang on to. And hope for. Then again, a normal person wouldn't know about the accident. Anya's family didn't talk about it. Even Chase only knew his cousin had been in some kind of a car accident. He didn't know she had caused it or that she hadn't been alone.

After the young country star had finished, to hugs and kisses from the bride and groom and enthusiastic applause from the audience, the band took a break and recorded music began to fill the air. The guests' happy voices lifted with praise for the song and for Lacey.

Poof. If Anya's one regret, the biggest, stupidest, most thoughtless mistake she'd ever made, were to be erased, two lives would drastically change for the better. But that was crazy. The woman had to be deranged, her brain affected by too much hair dye.

...Right?

Anya moved away from the table to melt into a throng of chattering people, her chin tucked, hair over her face. She floated around the edges of groups of people until she reached the person she sought. Emma.

Beaming, with the waning sunlight framing her dark blonde hair in a halo from behind, and diamond earrings shimmering at her ears, the bride looked gorgeous, happiness rolling from her in waves. Her new husband stood next to her, tall and proud.

Emma's gaze met Anya's. "Hi," the bride enthused. "Are you enjoying yourself? Wasn't Lacey great?"

"She was, but she had good material to work with. Love the song."

"Thanks. It's special to us."

"And everything's so beautiful. I'm glad I could be here."

Emma put a hand out to grasp Anya's. "I'm glad I got to meet you. You came a long way." Her touch was warm and genuine, a large ring sparkling on her third finger.

Another guest strode up to stand by Emma. "The blushing bride," he gushed, sending the aroma of freshly consumed beer into the air.

Emma turned, ready to greet him.

Anya didn't let her. "Excuse me," she said to the man, giving him an apologetic look. "I need to ask her something. Just one. Question." She put a finger up. "Won't take long. I promise."

He raised his eyebrows. "Sure thing. I need...you know, another beer, anyway." He lumbered off.

Emma's eyebrows went up, as well, but hers were concerned. "Is everything okay?"

Anya dropped her voice and leaned in closer. "Do you know someone who calls herself Madame Claire? Orange hair, smoker's voice, a strange sort of an accent?"

Emma's face paled. "I—um. Why do you ask?" She glanced over her shoulder, as if to reassure herself Chase was still there. He smiled at her and went back to talking with another guest.

"She said some things to me. Weird things."

Emma's head whipped back around to Anya. "What things? Never mind. Don't listen to her."

Not the reaction she'd expected. Anya's voice dropped to a whisper that only Emma was close enough to hear. "Is she crazy, or what?"

Emma took Anya's elbow to steer her a few feet away. "She's…eccentric. But otherwise, she's, you know, harmless." A beat passed. "Harmless *enough*."

Before Anya knew it, the words spilled out. "She says she can erase a mistake from my life. As if that could even happen." She hoped her cousin's bride wouldn't hear the insane hope lurking in her voice. "She wants me to meet with her to talk about it. What is this, a game? Or she's trying to sell me something?"

Emma's face turned white beneath her golden tan. She clutched Anya's upper arms. "Holy shit. Be careful with that stuff. *Very* careful."

CHAPTER TWO

The restaurant was easy to find. All Anya had to do was follow the smell of blueberry pancakes wafting through Maven, Ohio's Main Street. She looked at her watch. 8:58 a.m. She'd been insane to come here. Clearly.

She wouldn't have come if Emma hadn't reacted the way she had. She'd been sure Emma would say something along the lines of, *That's my aunt, she's not right in the head,* or *That's a woman I met and felt sorry for. I befriended her because no one else would.* Something, anything, other than warning Anya to stay away from Madame Claire *because* of what she had claimed she could do. And then not saying anything more.

Even the tiny possibility of having that one moment in time, that horrible accident, erased from her life was too tempting for Anya to let go. No one could actually do that. But what if this Madame Claire person *could*?

Anya leaned against the brick wall of the restaurant and squeezed her eyes shut while images from the night of the accident flashed through her mind. She and Ryder had been arguing at a basketball party, where he had had too much to drink. Too much to fend off the attentions of a very pretty, very determined cheerleader.

Anya had finally pushed him out of the apartment and into the passenger side of his car, her body shaking with jealousy, hurt, and anger. She knew he didn't drink often, that he wasn't thinking straight, that he had aimed faint protests at the other girl even as he smiled at her. She knew that rationally, but the part of her that had always been terrified she'd lose this man who held her heart in his hands had prevailed. By the time she'd taken the wheel, she'd been furious.

So furious she hadn't noticed she had only a green traffic light at the intersection, not a green arrow. Her hand was still on the left turn signal when the car she was driving slammed into one traveling straight through the intersection.

The rest was a blur. All of the horrible clanking, crunching sounds. The eerie quiet afterward, broken only by the sound of a hubcap rolling away, as everything settled.

Anya tried to call out for Ryder, panicking when he didn't answer, her voice scraping against her throat. She lay there, twisted, with one side of her head against the car door, her tears warm against her skin and stinging. Fear formed a painful lump she couldn't swallow away until before long, she couldn't swallow at all. Someone come, someone help us. Please, she implored the Heavens.

It didn't take long. She soon heard car doors slamming. Feet running. Sirens in the distance. She tasted blood and stale night air in her mouth.

In the hospital, she could only open one eye. A huge bandage on the side of her face prevented the other eye from doing much of anything. But she could see her parents standing at her bedside, their eyes wide and frightened, her mother clutching her purse like a lifeline. "Anya?" she'd managed to ask, as though she had to verify it was her kid.

Anya wanted to nod her head, but it hurt too much. She tried to ask about Ryder, but couldn't think how to form the words.

A police officer stood on the other side of her bed, his clothes dark blue and smelling like the dry cleaner, his badge shiny and his expression grim, a notepad and pen clutched in his fingers. "You're awake," he'd announced. "Want to tell me what happened?"

No. She didn't. She couldn't think about it. Because…because she couldn't.

What she wanted to do was cry. And she did, the salty tears stinging cuts on her cheeks and, on the unbandaged side, streaming down onto her neck.

She wanted her mother to put down her purse, hug her, and tell her everything would be okay. She wanted Ryder to come through the door and fold her in his safe, strong arms. She did *not* want to talk to a police officer.

But it turned out she didn't have a choice. And that's when her world fell apart. That's when she found out the accident had been her fault, that she'd hurt Ryder. Hurt him badly. Not long after, she'd learned he wouldn't walk again, let alone play basketball.

His dreams were over. She could still feel her hand on the turn signal, hear its relentless click, click, click. Feel the jealousy rising through her with the intensity of a rapidly moving fire, ready to devour everything in its path.

"You are coming inside or are you not?"

Anya swiped at her eyes and turned to the door of the restaurant, where Madame Claire stood, today attired in black, a friendlier color where orange hair was concerned. "I'm—I don't know," she answered.

"It is not all day I have."

"Me either. I have a plane to catch."

"Then you will come in. Because if you do not, your chance will be missed and when it is crying and carrying on you are doing, I will not answer the phone."

Anya straightened, pushing her shoulders into the brick wall. This woman knew nothing about her. "I don't carry on."

"Hmpf." The woman sniffed. "That we will see about."

"Fine. I'll come in. I'm hungry."

The two women stared each other down.

* * *

Claire shook her head, irritated. This, she did not have time for. "Please. No need to do me the favor." She led the way through the door, assuming the young woman would follow. It was not as though Claire was here by choice. But when it is your dead mother who calls in the middle of the night to tell you what you must do, there is nothing for it but to listen.

This girl, Claire had to help. This girl, she had a dangerous future.

No matter the spell had gone wrong before. More than once before. This time it would be right. Her mother had given her the *noteikt*, the fix. Too bad her mother could not have thought to give it before, but one must never that mind now.

Claire made her way to the table in the back of the restaurant, where she had placed her purse and black sweater. Anya followed and then sat across from her, eyes down. Like a scared rabbit, this girl was, Claire thought, clasping her hands in front of her.

The restaurant was busy this morning. Tables buzzed with conversation and the kitchen with the clanking of dishes, while the aroma of coffee, syrup, and blueberries punctuated the air. A talk show host on a TV mounted in one corner chattered with the news of the day, though no one in the restaurant appeared to be interested in what she had to say.

A waitress appeared at their table, notepad in her hand. Claire motioned her away. "We will talk first," she said to the woman. "Then you will bring us the blueberry pancakes."

Anya looked up. "And coffee, please. When you have a minute." She smiled.

"Sure thing." The waitress snapped her gum and walked away.

"I do not like the gum," said Claire.

Anya carefully unwrapped her silverware from the paper napkin, giving Claire a chance to take a good look at her. The young woman was a beauty, no doubt of that. Her face was long, her cheekbones high, her nose straight, her lashes thick and dark, and her brown hair shining with strands of gold. Her skin glowed and her eyes were a shade of blue that reminded Claire of the tanzanite stone on a necklace her mother had given her.

This woman, she could not walk by without people noticing. They would look, they would sigh. Maybe from envy, who knew? But that scar. It was wrong, as though someone had jabbed a wicked brush at a wet painting.

And all around her, a cloud of sadness. It was strange, the way this sadness clung to her. One could almost touch it, feel it stain the fingers.

She waited, until at last Anya's eyes rose to meet hers. Again, the images of a car accident floated around the edges of Claire's vision. It was dark. There was blood oozing. The side of her head hurt. She was not alone, but all alone. A passenger was not conscious and the quiet, it wrenched and tore at her.

Her shoulders began to sag with the weight of something remembered that would not let go. "This accident," Claire said. "It has caused you much pain."

Anya's gaze darted away and then back.

Claire concentrated on new images swirling before her. A handsome young man in a wheelchair, his anger steaming, hissing, boiling over. Pushing himself up, trying to walk. Instead falling and pounding the floor with his fist. "The man," she said. "He blames you for this accident."

"I didn't mean to do it," Anya whispered to the salt and pepper shakers.

Claire saw Anya before a mirror. Touching the scar. Yanking her hair into a high ponytail, her lips quivering. Now walking down a hallway in a place that looked like a hospital, stopping at the door of the man in the wheelchair. The smell of medicine and disinfectant pinched Claire's nostrils.

The man, he would not look at Anya. She tried to say something to him, but he threw a plastic bottle filled with water at the door. Anya cringed as it smacked the wood and then fell to the floor, wobbling away, leaving a trail of leaking water.

The sorrow that went through the woman, it stabbed so hard, it caused Claire to flinch. Ah, she had loved this man.

Anya looked up.

"What happened that night, it is your biggest regret."

"It was my fault." Again, in a whisper. Anya looked miserable. She brushed her hair back and lifted her chin, fully revealing her scar. "Could you just—change it so he didn't get hurt?"

"When I poof, I poof. Gone is this mistake."

The naked hope in Anya's eyes was almost too much for the psychic to bear. Guarantees, she did not have. After all, things had not gone as they should have when she'd done this spell in the past. Once again, she shook off the doubt. A psychic who did not believe in herself was useful to no one. Her mother had given her the fix. The bubble of dread inside her stomach, it must go away. *Now.*

The waitress set two mugs down and filled them with black coffee. To the rim, leaving no room for Claire's cherished cream and sugar. She aimed a displeased look at the woman who wore a nameplate that said *Christy*. A moment later, Christy put a plate of hot pancakes before each of them.

"Cream?" Claire asked of the waitress's back. No response. "She is on my list." She'd heard that saying somewhere and liked it. Grumbling under her breath, she pulled a pad of paper and a pencil from her purse, scribbled the name *Christy* on her new list, and then wondered what to do with it.

Anya leaned over to another table, bringing back a small metal pitcher of cream.

"Very good," Claire murmured. She ripped the edge of a sugar packet and put the contents in her mug, then took a big enough drink of the coffee, twisting her mouth at the bitter taste, to leave room for her cream. She turned back to the young woman before her. "Tell me, what work is it you do?" She cut into the stack of pancakes and took a bite, letting the sweetness of the warm blue fruit linger on her tongue.

Anya traced a pattern in the table with one finger. "I'm an assistant. To an actress. In L.A."

"Ah." Claire did not have to say anything more. It would come.

"It's an okay job."

"Sure."

"Nobody looks at an assistant, so they don't ask what happened."

"Is rude," Claire murmured.

"Is life." Anya's cheeks pinked. "I mean, it's not as though it matters."

"You do not matter?"

"That's not what I meant." She hesitated. "Or maybe it was."

Claire was certain of that much. "This job, you like it?"

"I'm good at it."

"Different question, that one."

Anya sucked in a breath, thinking. "It's okay. The pay is fine and she's not as demanding as some. She likes the spotlight and I don't. So it works."

"You would miss this job if you didn't have it?" Claire's mother had warned her that one never knew how a life, after the change, would turn out. For some, new mistakes would be made that were bigger than the one that had been erased.

A shrug. "Probably not."

Such unhappiness, this one. Yet she seemed to put her arms around the sadness and hold it close to her. "What is it this scar on your face," she gestured toward the other woman's cheek, "keeps you from doing?"

"Nothing."

"The truth, please."

Anya's finger stilled, though she continued to focus on the table. "As I said, I don't like being in the spotlight, so I'm doing what works."

"What if you *did* like, as you say, the spotlight?"

Silence. Claire worried that her pancakes would grow cold.

At last, the other woman replied, "I would do something in fashion. Styling. Maybe some modeling." She said it with apology in her voice. "Someone once told me I could be a model, if it weren't for…this." She touched her scar, but dropped her fingers back down quickly, as if they'd been burned. "Probably not true, but I guess you never know."

"This is good." Surprising, maybe, as she did not see this girl in that world. Her clothes looked made to lurk in the shadows, not stand out. But okay, there was something else for her but the assisting of an actress. "Fashion. This is something you like?"

The woman's face changed, softening and taking on a cautious hope. "It's art, really. I was the one all my friends asked to help them with their outfits. I put things together they never would have thought of. They loved what I picked out."

Claire took in the woman's plain black shirt, jeans, and lack of jewelry. "You do this now?"

Anya looked up, meeting Claire's eyes. "Sometimes for the actress I work for, though she has a stylist she uses most of the time."

Other images were floating through Claire's mind. Detailed sketches—of people, their faces, of landscapes. "There is other art you do."

The woman's face changed, shutting down. "Not any more."

There was a lot this Anya no longer did, Claire suspected. Yet another image slid across Claire's vision, one of a despondent Anya eyeing a bottle of pills. Crying until the tears no longer came and her shoulders shook with a dry, piercing pain of body and heart. This, then, was the dangerous future she had sensed for this girl. She could not let this happen. "Why did you give up on this?"

Anya appeared to consider the question, but then abruptly changed the subject, her mouth twisting. "How much is this 'poofing' going to cost me?"

Claire put her fork down. "You will not pay," she said, steepling her fingers. "It is the last time I will do such a thing. All will go well and then my mother, she will quit with calling me to say how I do it wrong." It was why she had said yes when her mother said this woman, this Anya, was the one who needed her. A person needed to sleep at night.

Her mother, calling during the three a.m. portal opening few knew about and even fewer on the other end could hear, did not help with that sleep. Until she got this right, her mother, who had been so much better at the spell, would not let her alone.

But now Claire knew there was more to the spell. Better the late than not ever.

Anya's eyes narrowed. "Why me?"

Suspicious, this one. "Is it always this way with the questions when someone brings you a gift?"

"A gift," Anya repeated. She looked to be trying the words out, turning them around in her head, deciding whether she liked them.

Claire drained half of the coffee in her mug. "I return to Seattle today. My plane, it leaves this afternoon." She watched the struggle between wanting to believe and not wanting to believe play out in the other woman's eyes. "It is simple, this poof." Not so, but Anya would know no differently.

"And he—I mean, no one, will ever know it used to be different?"

"No one. In the matter of fact, you are not to tell anyone or all could unravel most unpredictably. This is important. Do you understand?"

"Not really." She looked confused.

Claire struggled with her patience. She wanted to eat her pancakes, but was not one to talk with food in her mouth. The spell would not take long. "It is easy, this. I poof, you do not tell anyone, I do not tell anyone, my mother does not tell anyone."

"I don't know, it sounds—"

"You have one chance. Now is this chance." A person had only so much patience and could only be expected to put off blueberries so long.

"Fine." Anya appeared to have reached a decision. "Go ahead. Please." She straightened her shoulders, as though bracing for the worst. "And thank you. I think."

Claire nodded. "You are welcome."

"What do I need to do?"

"You will sit. Then you will leave. And when you do, when you leave this place, your life will be as it is on *this same day*, without this mistake in your past."

"And Ryd—the man in the accident?"

"I have already said, have I not?" Too much time, this was taking. Claire had to eat before she made the long drive to the airport or her stomach would make the loud sound that told everyone she was hungry. That sound, she did not like.

"Right." Anya moved her plate aside and locked her fingers together. Waiting.

Claire looked from one side to the other, and, confident no one was looking or interested, raised her hands and began to murmur the words of the spell. Her concentration wavered as she saw Anya close her eyes. She felt the hope coming from the young woman in waves so strong, they nearly toppled Claire. Where was she? *Ah, yes.*

An aroma, strong and sweet, floated to her nose. Claire opened one eye. The waitress Christy was walking past, her arms weighed down with more pancakes. The blueberries. How wonderful they smelled. She was sure her own had gone cold, but perhaps they would still taste good.

Quickly, she finished the spell so she could find out. Then she lowered her hands to the table.

Anya stared at her. "I don't feel anything."

"You will not. Yet. As I said, when you leave."

The younger woman rose slowly from her seat, pulled out her wallet, removed a twenty-dollar bill, and set it on the table. "That's for my breakfast," she said. She hesitated. "Thank you. For—I'm not sure." And then she was gone, the bell on the glass front door tinkling over her head.

The waitress Christy looked up at the door, but not seeing anything or anyone, turned back to pouring coffee for her customers.

Claire nodded quietly to herself and took a bite of her cold pancakes. She hoped life would now go well for this Anya. If it didn't, Claire's mother would never let her forget it.

She motioned Christy over and put in a new order for hot blueberry pancakes. The waistline, what did she care, at this moment?

CHAPTER THREE

Anya Ramsey was having a not-so-great day.

The lashes above her right eye insisted on sticking together, she had a zit ready to break through the layers of makeup on her face, and because she'd splurged on a bowl of ice cream last night, the client's dress was a little too tight for Anya to breathe comfortably. Or really, if she had to be truthful, hardly at all.

It was cool for a February day in Los Angeles, only in the fifties. She had to mentally will the goose bumps away and that wasn't working real well.

On top of that, she had, from out of nowhere, acquired a spring-action reflex that had her ducking her chin and sending her hair forward at random, turning the photographer's day into a bad one as well. He wasn't the most patient guy to begin with.

"What the hell are you *doing*?" he yelled. "What is with that hair? Keep your goddamn chin up!"

"Sorry," Anya said for the fifth time. He wasn't responding to her go-to apology expression—a mix of contrition and concern.

She wished *she* knew what the hell her chin was doing. Zest—the online fashion retailer she worked for—frequently used her as a model for fashion shoots and she'd never before had any problems. Even the most demanding photographers relaxed around her. "There's something about you," her boss had mused. "You're just so *happy*. Or something."

Anya hadn't been one hundred percent sure that was a compliment, but she'd decided to take it as one.

She concentrated hard on keeping her chin up and her hair back, letting her fingers float through the strands, oozing confidence and tranquility, as though she could not think of a single better thing in life than wearing this brand-new designer's edgy clothing while leaning against a building rooftop's crumbling half wall.

But then, balancing on six-inch heels only slightly bigger than a pencil, with toes that came to a point so sharp they could qualify as a weapon, while wearing a close-fitting white silk dress that exploded at the neck in a frenzy of color was, admittedly, a pretty great time, even with the zit, sticky eyelashes, and tighter-than-tight waist.

She took half a breath. No more ice cream. Ever.

The photographer moved closer, clicking off shots. He was somewhere around fifty, but looked closer to seventy, with sun-toughened skin, nicotine-stained fingers, and gray hair that curled in some places and not in others. Anya expelled the little breath allowed her. The sun was relentless today and the photographer didn't appear to be a big fan of deodorant, so breathing out was preferable to breathing in.

"Chin up," he barked.

She obeyed, doing her best to ignore the sinking feeling that she had even less control over the unstable wall when she couldn't see it.

"Up, up, up!"

Rocks shifted against her calves, but she stretched her chin up until she felt like a deranged ostrich. She held her breath, wishing there were some sort of padding in the silk dress to help cushion the fall that had to be coming. Would the photographer call for help or click off action shots of her tumbling toward the ground while yelling for her to extend her neck? The latter, probably.

After several more shots, he grunted, "That's it."

It, as in done for today? Or as in done for *forever*? No matter how many times she did this, she continued to nurse the fear that one day someone would call her out as a fraud, nothing more than a model wannabe.

Anya tensed, her gaze flickering toward the nervous designer standing a few feet away. He clasped his palms together and closed his eyes, apparently sending a prayer to the fashion gods.

The photographer clicked through shots on his camera. "Good," he said. "That works."

Anya's body relaxed. One pencil point heel began to turn the wrong way, but she caught herself in time and pulled it back, a bright smile on her face. Apparently these shoes required a permanent state of tension, along with a nearly impossible sense of balance. "Great!" she enthused.

The photographer turned away to begin stowing his equipment and Anya's eyes zeroed in on a tattoo on his neck. A jagged black outline about four inches long. A bolt of lightning.

There was something disturbingly familiar about it, though she couldn't figure out what it was. A zipper gone wrong? A zig-zag road somewhere. Or—a wound. A *wound*? Her heartbeat sped up and she felt seasick. The image blurred. Anya put a hand out to steady herself, hearing, as if from a distance away, pieces of rock crumble to her feet.

She tried to avert her eyes, but couldn't. The tattoo morphed into something else, something that stabbed at her in a series of rapid-fire pricks. The image faded, lessening the pain, then abruptly sharpened. She put a hand to her cheek, feeling something sear her skin. *What the—?*

"Is she okay?" she heard the designer ask. He sounded nervous.

The photographer turned again and straightened, a question on his face.

Anya lost sight of the tattoo.

The dizziness stopped and she felt heat crawl up into her cheeks. Strange. "Did you get everything you needed?" she asked, infusing her smile with a full dose of eagerness-to-please. She had to be the model everyone wanted to work with. She *had* to be.

He hesitated and then responded with a gruff, "Yeah." The corners of his mouth turned up, seemingly despite his best intentions.

The designer clapped. "Yay," he bleated.

The photographer turned and his tattoo moved back into Anya's field of vision. The dizziness returned, this time with a slow motion video clip that started, buffered, started again. She saw herself before a mirror, touching a similarly shaped scar. On her cheek.

The image was so vivid, so real, that her knees gave way and her right shoe/weapon skittered out from under her. Anya's hand slapped the half wall for support, her hip scraping against it. Right before she fell, the photographer was at her side to grab her arm, lifting her upward and away from the wall. Anya stumbled again then righted herself.

"You all right?"

Her palms and hip stung and she didn't even want to think about the rocks she heard hitting pavement below. "Sure. Yes, fine."

But she wasn't. Not at all. Her hand flew to her face as panic shot through her. "Are you going to remove this in the photo?" she asked, rubbing her fingers across the skin of her cheek.

The photographer narrowed his eyes. "Remove what?"

Anya rubbed harder. "This— Can't you see it? This *thing*."

The photographer released her arm and stepped back. "I don't know what you're talking about."

That made two of them. "Uh…nothing. Sorry. You know, it's just—" She dragged her hair forward to cover her cheek, knowing, even as she did it, that she didn't have a reason to. "I have to leave." She began hurrying away as fast as the dagger heels would allow, which made for a stumble-walk-stumble that couldn't be pretty.

He'd think she was crazy, but that might be the least of her problems at the moment.

She had an overwhelming sense of occupying someone else's body, a disconnection. Something about her face wasn't right. It might have been right when she'd started this shoot, but it wasn't now. Which made no sense, but the feeling refused to go away.

An assistant stood by to help her down the stairs and into a small room where she could change out of the clothing and back into her own. As soon as the dress had been unzipped, she scooted it off her body and opened the door to hand it to the assistant, who would ensure its safe return to the designer.

She moved to the mirror, peering at her reflection and pulling at the skin of her cheek. Nothing. But there had to be. She'd *felt* it. She pressed a hand to her forehead, trying to remember back a few minutes ago to what she'd felt. That tattoo had started it all, with its jagged, unforgiving edges. Like a sword had sliced through skin.

Or metal. *Metal?* What the hell. This day kept getting weirder.

Anya's cell rang. She tore her gaze from the mirror to glance at the caller ID, then braced herself before she answered. "Hi, Mom."

"Oh good, you can talk. Seems as though that hardly ever happens these days."

Anya caught her sigh before her mother could hear it. "How's the wedding?"

"Lovely. We're at the reception. I wish you could have been here."

"Me, too." She adored her cousin Chase, but this photo shoot had been an opportunity she couldn't afford to turn down. She wedged the phone between her shoulder and her chin and reached for her jeans.

"I have something to tell you."

Anya stopped midway through pulling on her jeans. "What? Is it Dad?" Before the photo shoot had come up, Anya had been the one supposed to fly from L.A. to Ohio to represent the family at the wedding. Her father's recent heart attack had scared them into thinking it might not be good for him to travel. Her mother, though, wasn't one to go alone.

"No." Her mother's voice took on a familiar tinny note. "But he can't overdo it or he'll be right back in the hospital."

"It's good you're there to tell him that."

A beat of silence. Then her mother said, "I ran into Karla Brandt right before we left. At the grocery store, of all places."

Anya's heart sank.

"Did you hear me? Ryder's mother."

"I know who she is." Anya's voice was quiet.

"I was surprised, I'll tell you that. The last time I saw her was at the hospital. You know. That time."

Anya squeezed her eyes shut. *Don't say it. Please. Don't say* that time *you put him in a wheelchair for life, while you came away without a scratch.*

"She came up to me to ask how you are."

Even though Anya's eyes were closed, she could clearly picture her mother and Ryder's mother awkwardly meeting by the dairy section ten years after the accident that had changed everything for the Brandt family.

Wait a minute. Something was wrong about this conversation, a feeling, a thought she couldn't pinpoint. It hovered in the air, just out of her reach. Ryder. Something about Ryder wasn't right…

"I told her you're doing well, what with that place you work for."

That place. *Zest*, the hottest, most fabulous online retailer in the industry right now. Anya was standing on the fashion zip-line platform, ready to soar, loving her job and knowing full well that there were at least a thousand other girls who would kill to have it. While Ryder remained in the grip of a wheelchair. Thanks to his one-time girlfriend.

"She was glad to hear things have worked out so well for you."

Ow. The arrow hit its mark, sharp and precise. "That's nice of her."

"She's a very nice woman, Anya." It sounded like a reprimand.

"Yes, she is."

"Don't you wonder how her son is doing? I know I did."

I know exactly how Ryder is doing. "How is he?" she asked her mother, because it would be harder to explain why she *wasn't* asking.

"Karla says he's doing very well. He's the basketball coach at Conner High School now. He teaches history there, too."

And runs a kids' basketball camp in the summer. "That's good to hear." She zipped up her jeans and reached for the new lace top she never would have been able to afford if it hadn't been for her employee discount.

"I just think it's good he isn't being…limited."

Anya quickly filled in the subtext: *Because of what you did to him.* "I have to go, Mom." *Will you ever forgive me for making one horrible mistake?*

"I know you're busy." *I can't forgive you.*

"Give Chase and Dad a hug for me." *I can't talk about it any more.*

"I will." *Neither can I.*

CHAPTER FOUR

Anya awoke in a panic. She'd been dreaming. It had been bad. She pushed herself up on the bed, leaning on the palms of her hands and blinking hard to orient herself.

Her heart raced until her throat threatened to close. The accident. It had replayed in her mind in excruciating detail. From the sickening thuds and crunches to her relief that the driver of the other car had suffered only bruises to the devastating news that Ryder had been paralyzed.

In the dream, she'd fallen to the pavement and the paramedics, nodding their heads as if to say it was only what she deserved, had stepped away, leaving her alone.

Her cheek, though. It had bled. A lot. In a trail of red that rushed from her face to stream across the yellow traffic line in the street. She'd watched it in wonder, certain that somehow, she should stop all that blood from leaving her body. Gas fumes stung her nostrils and made her stomach queasy.

Ryder. Where was he? They'd taken him away from her in an ambulance, its siren piercing the night air.

She had to follow, had to know he was all right. But everyone had ignored her and her legs felt too weak to move.

Then, from out of nowhere, a woman with orange hair had materialized to stand over her. "Poof!" she said. Agitated, she repeated the word, with obvious frustration this time. *"Poof!"*

The bleeding had stopped. Anya lifted her head from the pavement and touched her cheek. Nothing. Then she'd scrambled to her feet and run after the ambulance, calling for Ryder until her throat grew raw. The paramedics wouldn't stop. She kept running until her chest burned and her cries caught deep in her throat.

She'd forced herself to awaken by gritting her teeth and repeating, "Wake up" over and over, each time with more urgency.

Anya moved her legs to the side of the bed and stood. She ran a hand through her hair, feeling its reluctance to loosen from the damp sweat on her face. Groggy, but relieved to be awake and no longer in the throes of the dream, she made her way to the shower and turned on the water.

Once she'd stripped off her pajamas, she left them in a pile and walked into the shower, immersing herself in the warm, streaming water, hoping it would wash away the memory of the dream and send it spiraling down the drain. This was real life, not dream life. *Thank God.* She poured shampoo into her hand and rubbed it across her scalp, working it into a furious lather.

That orange-haired woman. The blood pouring from Anya's cheek. It didn't make sense, which wasn't unusual for dreams, but it had all been so vivid, had seemed so real.

Anya closed her eyes, tipped her head and rinsed the shampoo from her hair. It had to have been her guilt from the accident, manifesting itself in a new way. The burden had been with her for so long, it sat like a lead weight on her shoulders. It was by now such a familiar part of her, she wouldn't feel anchored to the ground were it ever to lift.

She'd only gone to see Ryder once in the rehab facility and the experience had been so devastating, she had never returned. She hadn't been able to look him in the eyes, hadn't wanted to see in them what he had to be thinking—that she'd emerged from the accident she'd caused without a scratch while he'd lost the future he'd dreamt of since he was a kid.

He'd been quiet. She'd blubbered her apologies, swiped a hand at her eyes and nose, and walked over to a window to stare out it, unseeing. When Ryder had tried to offer his own apology, she'd cut him off, her own guilt so all consuming, it left no room for anything else.

She'd given him a quick, hard hug, leaving her tears and mascara on his shirt, and said goodbye. With a finality they both recognized, though neither acknowledged.

Anya hadn't been able to stay at the university. She'd transferred to one in another town, where no one knew what she'd done. Where no one would whisper about her.

One moment she and Ryder had been in love, the kind of love that filled her entire soul. The next, it was if they were separately tripping over branches in a pitch-black forest, without a compass, deaf to the other's voice. Unable to find their way back to each other. Unable to even try, if the truth be told.

She hated that truth.

When she'd started dating again, she'd made sure they weren't the kind of guys she'd get too attached to. That kind of love didn't only hurt when you screwed up, but it also sliced you to pieces. Left a permanent scar on the inside, where no one could see it.

Ha. That could be it. She'd dreamt about having a wound that *could* be seen. Only fitting, after all.

Anya let the water stream over her head and down her body. Her parents would be on their way back today from the wedding. She wished she could have gone. She would have liked seeing Chase so happy. He was a good guy; he deserved someone as great as his Emma.

With a sigh, she turned off the water, dried off, wrapped a towel around her head, and put on her fluffy white robe. Before she got dressed, it was time to be…(she always felt as though there should be a drum roll) *Annie*.

Annie Sterling, fellow teacher, dog lover, basketball fan. A woman who had developed an intense online relationship with Ryder Brandt.

A few months ago, she'd heard the song "We Belong Together." The one that had been playing, weeks before the accident, when she and Ryder reconciled after breaking up for two days because the depth of what they felt scared both of them.

The words had taken her straight back to her dorm room, to the tears rolling down her cheeks as Mariah sang, "I should've held on tight, I never should've let you go." To Ryder catching her tears with his finger and then folding her in his arms, whispering they'd never be apart again.

And the same ache in her throat, the one that had been there that night years ago, had returned. Zeke, the guy she'd been with when the song played at the bar, had thought she was upset because she'd just found out, with a glance at his phone when it pinged, that he'd been cheating on her.

That wasn't it. She'd pretty much expected Zeke to cheat on her from the time they'd first gone out. He was handsome, self-obsessed, and winked a lot, at her and at other women, as if he knew something no one else did. He was a cardboard cutout of all the men she'd dated over the last several years. Intimacy that wasn't intimate. Conversation that hummed along at the surface level. Fun that wasn't joyful.

And fuck it all, everything had been going exactly as planned until Zeke had decided to be an ass at the exact moment the song had brought back memories too painful to face.

"C'mon. You can't expect me to save all this," he gestured at his crotch, "for only one woman." An imploring grin.

She'd shot back with, "There isn't even enough there for *one*, you asshole." Ryder had once told her she was his sun, moon, and stars. Zeke had just told her to get in line.

No, the tears in her eyes hadn't been about Zeke. She wanted Ryder back in her life, even at a distance. If she could only connect with him again, a part of her might be able to heal. Her heart might not suffer freezer burn when she was with someone like Zeke.

So she'd become someone else—at least online. Annie Sterling, a woman who had moved from southern California to live in upstate New York. And she'd friended Ryder on Facebook. To see what would happen.

It had been easy to do, which was an unsettling feeling she ignored, for the most part. The photo she used was one of her coworker and friend Caitlin, who had agreed, after grilling Anya, it wasn't *that* bad an idea. Another friend, Sarah, was an elementary school teacher. Anya spent enough time with her, absorbing information, to be able to pull off a passable imitation of a working teacher. And Anya's own dog, Bo, a rescued yellow Lab, affably filled in as his real self.

At first, Anya had felt bad about the lies. She'd told herself how wrong it was to do this. She'd told herself that right up until the time Ryder answered and they started messaging, emailing, and then texting regularly. They'd even talked on the phone a few times, where Anya adopted a slightly higher version of her own voice, to make sure he didn't recognize her. He didn't, but then, it had been years since he'd heard her speak.

The connection became like a drug. The more interaction with him, the more elated she felt, even as she berated herself for the deception. A niggling voice inside her told her that if she couldn't be Anya, the relationship wasn't worth having.

She quit listening to that voice and it became harder and harder to let go of Ryder.

Being Annie felt good. Probably because Annie was not the kind of person to cause a horrible car wreck. Annie didn't make stupid mistakes. Annie's students, their parents, and her dog adored her and it wasn't just for what she looked like. She made sure of that in the stories she told Ryder.

She wished she really *was* Annie. But at least for a part of the day, she could be.

She folded the soft terry cloth robe up around her shoulders and let one pink slipper dangle from her foot as she settled into the comfy, overstuffed armchair and picked up her phone. There it was. A text from Ryder. *Ready for another day of shaping young minds?* An emoticon next to the words winked broadly.

Hell, yes, she wrote back. *They are, after all, the future.*

God help us, he said. *Head underground now. Take Bo.*

Anya smiled. She hesitated, just for a moment, before responding. *Such optimism so early in the morning.*

A quick reply. *Didn't sleep great. Spent the night thinking about you.*

An even bigger smile. *Thinking what about me?*

She waited with nervous anticipation. It took a full minute for his next text to appear. *About things that don't involve sleep. Meet me in person and I'll show you.*

Anya pictured his handsome face, and how disappointed and angry he would be if he found out who she really was. *Make it a promise,* she typed. *But right now, you'd better get ready to influence future world leaders. Playoffs start tonight?*

Promise. And yes. Playoff tonight. Wish us luck.

Okay, luck. But you won't need it. Kick some ass!

Could be tough. Kicking leg not working.

Oh shit. Anya gulped. *Then roll over 'em,* she typed.

Will do. This thing is a bitch if you get caught beneath the wheels.

She laughed out loud, causing Bo to raise and tip his head in a question. *And stay with the Flex Offense. The boys are executing great.*

They are. Thanks. Hope I can concentrate on the game. There's this beautiful girl I can't stop thinking about.

Anya's smile spread so wide, it actually hurt. *Really. Who is she? She'd better not be messing with my man.* She'd never called him her man before. Her smile faded and she chewed on a fingernail, waiting for his reply.

It was quick. *Oh, she's messing with him all right. Dreams like you wouldn't believe. Had to take a cold shower in the middle of the night.*

She paused, finger over the keys, and then typed, *I would believe. Having those same dreams.* The memories of being with Ryder, of him making wild and tender love to her, were still heart-achingly vivid.

The ones where I hold you, stroke you, and love you for days, like you've never been loved? Shit, Annie. When are we going to meet? This is killing me.

Love. He'd said it. Maybe not as in, "I love you." But he'd still said it. Tears pricked at the back of her eyes. *Soon,* she promised. How she would make good on that, she had no idea. But maybe it could happen. Maybe everything could somehow, someway, be okay.

I'm holding you to that.

Anya stood, pulled the towel from her head and shook her damp hair free. When she reached the bathroom mirror, she realized she was still smiling. Ryder's messages had that effect on her.

She stared into her reflection. She could meet him in person. Sure she could. If she dyed her hair, wore brown contact lenses, and had plastic surgery to give her an entirely different smile. A Caitlin smile.

Who was she kidding? She could do all that and Ryder would still know her. She hoped so, anyway. At one time, he'd known everything there was to know about her.

Her cell rang. Her heart skipped a beat, hoping it would be Ryder, before she glanced at the caller ID. Zeke. She meant to press ignore, but her damp finger slipped on the screen and pressed accept. Great.

He spoke before she could even get out a hello. "Hey, babe."

"What is it, Zeke." Her voice was flat, disinterested.

His smooth voice just about melted the phone. "Ah now, Anya. Don't be mad. I can't take it when you're mad at me."

"I'm not mad at you." She didn't want to waste the time.

"That was mean, what you said to me. Good thing I know you didn't mean it."

She pictured his face puckering on the other side of the phone. He looked like a pouting little boy when he was trying to get his way, a technique she suspected he'd successfully used since he was a toddler. "Oh, I meant it." Not that she was proud of it. If there's one thing she prided herself on, it was not being mean. So much for that where Zeke was concerned.

"Right." He snorted. "You don't sound happy I called."

She wasn't going to play the pout-and-make-up game. She switched into her professional voice. "What can I do for you, Zeke?"

"Now you're talking. How about you let me take you out for dinner tonight? You pick the restaurant."

And after dinner, they would go to his apartment, where they would drink a nice bottle of wine and end up on his 1000 thread count Egyptian cotton sheets for a perfectly fine, if a little selfish on his part, night of sex. She would leave around midnight, tiptoeing out while he raised his hand in a sleepy goodbye. She never stayed all night. Never.

She almost said yes, as she had several times before. Dinner, wine, sex, with a good-looking man. Why the hell not? Did the cheating really matter?

It did. She pulled the cell away, staring at it. She could hear Zeke asking, "Anya? Are you there?"

"Sorry. No."

"So you're busy. Tomorrow then."

"No. Not tomorrow, either." She might be crazy, turning Zeke down. But she wasn't, and she knew it. It wasn't enough. What he had to offer wasn't enough. Not any more.

As she blew her hair dry, she found herself longing to see Ryder, hear his voice. As she applied her makeup, she berated herself for even considering it as a possibility. As she got dressed, she vowed never to contact him again, to make Annie Sterling disappear like the figment of Anya's imagination she was.

And as she took Bo for his morning walk, she wondered if Ryder could have a change of heart and be able to forgive her for what had happened. If he could want Anya instead of Annie.

When she and Bo returned, she hung up his leash and gave him a big goodbye-for-now hug. He settled into his dog bed with a satisfied sigh.

By the time Anya left the apartment, closing the door and locking it behind her, she'd decided she had to try to see Ryder as herself, as Anya. Even the thought of doing that sent shivers of apprehension up her spine. Could she roll her guilt down the virtual hill like the hundred pound boulder it was? Could he absolve her for what she'd done to him? Not likely.

But the thought of *not* trying made her entire body ache with sadness, with a yearning that pierced her soul. It had been years; maybe things were different now. She could try. Once. It would either be an air ball or a game winning three-pointer.

Either way, she'd pick herself up off the floor and go on.

Or not.

CHAPTER FIVE

Anya arrived at the last place on earth she'd thought she could allow herself to be. Yet, she'd even left work early to get here, and had taken pains to disguise her appearance until ready to reveal who she really was. *If*, and it was a big if, she could find the nerve. She could only hope the nerve she found didn't run screaming from her when she needed it most.

She followed the crowd into the Conner High School Wildcats gym, where the first playoff game, against the Moro High School Bears, was being held. As soon as she breathed in the scent of sweat, disinfectant, and old socks and heard the sharp squeaks of sneakers against the polished wood, she felt transported back to her own high school, where she'd spent way too many hours to count as a cheerleader.

For just an instant, she had a pang of longing for the simpler times when math homework and the ability to perform a backflip had been her biggest problems. But a person couldn't stay in high school forever.

She'd tucked her hair beneath a hoodie, and worn eyeglasses with black frames to help hide the oddly colored blue eyes that people said were her most distinctive feature. Her heart hammered so hard at the thought of seeing Ryder, of talking with him, and what might happen as a result, that she could hear it in her ears.

Good thing heart attacks didn't happen to people so young. Wait…did they? She could hear the newscaster now. "In sad news tonight, a young woman had to be taken from the Conner High School gym by ambulance and later passed away from what doctors are calling, Death by Rejection Anticipation. It's a new phenomenon likely to now be called Anya Ramsey Syndrome, and known for its highly preventable nature." She could hear him sigh. "Just don't make stupid mistakes, people, and you won't ever have to worry about contracting it."

It wasn't too late to back out. Yes, it was. No, it wasn't.

She attached herself to the edges of a group of people so the casual observer wouldn't realize she wasn't one of them. People were talking so animatedly to each other, they didn't even notice her. Wildcats parents, keyed up for the game.

Then she saw Ryder at the edge of the floor, his hands gripping the wheels of his chair, his attention locked on the players practicing in front of him. He called out an instruction to his point guard, who turned and zeroed in on his coach's words.

Oh God. Ryder. All grown up, into a confident, handsome man. And sexy as hell.

Shielded by a group of parents, Anya found a spot in the bleachers on the Conner side of the gym, behind a very tall man she could peek around. He probably had a son on the team. She sat on a message scrawled into the scarred wood that read, *Will you go to prom with me?* It looked to have been there for years. She wondered what the answer had been and whether they'd had a good time at prom.

A woman and her young kids sat down next to the tall man, juggling hot dogs and pop, and chattering with excitement.

A few minutes later, the game was underway. Though shrill whistles pierced through the action of running and pounding feet, Anya's attention focused on only one person, drinking in every detail of him like someone dying of thirst.

Ryder's once-lanky teenage body was now muscular, filling out the dark suit jacket he wore with a blue button-down shirt and a tie in the school colors of blue and green. His arms were strong, his fingers commanding as he easily moved the wheelchair back and forth, up and down the court sidelines, until you forgot it wasn't actually a part of his body.

She could not tear her eyes away from him.

The game turned intense, with only two points separating the Wildcats and their biggest rival. The Moro Bears grabbed the lead with seconds to go in the second quarter. Tension rippled through the crowd.

Then it was halftime and Ryder's wheelchair sped across the floor after his team. She said a silent prayer that his pep talk and adjustments would work. She knew how much the game meant to Ryder and his kids. She'd done her research. Moro had beaten the Conner Wildcats the last five years straight and won bragging rights they regularly exercised.

Anya took advantage of his brief absence from the gym to stand and stretch, pushing back her hoodie to look around at Ryder's new home. Typical gym, with high rafters to catch the crowd's yells of support, the clock with its protective cage, the electronic scoreboard. A huge, sixties-era graphic of a wildcat painted on one wall.

"Do you have someone on the team?"

Anya turned toward the voice, an older woman sitting a foot or so from her. "Um, no, just really like high school basketball." She mentally kicked herself as soon as the words were out. She should have made up a fictional brother or nephew, something.

The woman, who had one of those pleasant faces and eyes that crinkled when she smiled, murmured and nodded. "Oh."

"Well, you know, it's the playoffs and that's always a pretty big deal." She was only making it worse. Putting on her brightest smile, she asked, "You?"

"My son. Number twenty-five."

"Oh, right." Anya pushed her glasses up higher on her nose. "I noticed him. Great player."

"Thank you." The woman beamed. "We're very proud of him."

Anya put her hands in the pockets of her hoodie, striving for a casual pose. "And the coach, is he pretty good? Does your son like him?"

"Coach B is wonderful. Michael and the other boys have so much respect for him. He really knows the game and he's great with the kids."

"That's good," Anya said. "I've heard that about him." She was proud on Ryder's behalf.

The woman's voice dropped to confiding level. "Michael had a little trouble early on, keeping up with his homework while being at practices, but Coach B worked with him and now he's doing just fine."

"That's the best kind of a coach to have. One who knows it's not only about the sport."

"Isn't that the truth," the woman agreed. "Oh. Here they come."

The gym doors opened. Anya pulled her hoodie back into place and sat back down on the wooden seat. The teams again took the court, to wild cheers from parents and students.

"Number twenty-five," the woman reminded her, pointing at the court.

"Right there. I see him." Anya nodded and flashed another smile. The kid Ryder had worked with to make sure he could keep up with his homework.

Her eyes, though, were on Ryder, surrounded by his players. He looked so confident as a leader. In his element, in control. Her heart lifted. He'd found his passion. Without warning, she flashed back to the rehab center. He'd been calm and in control then. She'd been a hot mess. A coward.

She put her head in her hands and shoved the flashback aside, into a mental drawer she locked with a key. Then she turned her attention back to the action on the court, applauding along with the crowd until her palms stung.

The third quarter was close and hard-fought, but Conner took the lead, only to lose it again a few minutes later.

By the fourth quarter, Anya had her fists clenched in front of her face as her gaze darted from Ryder to the court and back again. He leaned forward, calling instructions to his players. The crowd, including Anya, rose to its feet. Next to her, the mother of number twenty-five gripped her hands in what looked like a prayer.

The scoreboard clock ticked off the remaining seconds in neon orange. Anya also clasped her hands together, hoping for a high school miracle. *Ryder has to win, he has to win. Please.*

She watched him, every fiber of his being concentrating on his players, urging them on. A Bears player bent his knees and sent the ball sailing toward the basket in a perfect arc. The crowd, on both sides, held its breath.

The perfect arc ended short, the ball bouncing off the rim of the hoop. Then a Wildcats player leapt up to grab the ball, hugging it to his chest. Anya joined the crowd in a scream. The neon orange numbers continued to tick as the player threw the ball down the court to his teammate, who stopped at the three-point line and, with Bears players racing toward him, took the shot. The clock hit zero at the same time the ball landed in the basket with a swish no one heard because the crowd had erupted with joy.

A Wildcats win, by one point.

Anya jumped up and down, along with the others watching. She and number twenty-five's mother slapped hands.

It was a huge victory for Ryder and his team. He'd shown what he could do as a coach and she was filled with pride for him. She wanted to tell everyone around her that she knew him, that he was the best, that she'd always known he would succeed, that she just didn't know it would be this way. But she should have.

She didn't say anything.

Anya peered through the parents hugging each other to see Ryder pumping his fists high in the air. His players swarmed him, hugging their coach and each other, until she couldn't see Ryder at all.

Tears pricked at Anya's eyes. She wanted, with every bit of her, to be a part of his world again. It was now or never. She shook her head and the hoodie fell back, away from her face. In an instant, her mind shot to the two of them together, his strong arms wrapped around her, holding her tight, skin to skin in a bed damp with their lovemaking, a breeze through an open window ruffling the curtain and dancing over the two of them, her cheeks burning pink from the stubble of whiskers across his chin.

Not that she'd thought about a reunion in any detail.

Shielded by the group standing and excitedly talking in the seats in front of her, she reached into her bag, pulling out a brush, a small mirror, and the black leather booties with nearly four-inch heels she'd splurged on because they looked so good with the skinny jeans she was wearing.

She peeked around the tall man to locate Ryder. He was still on the court, encircled by those congratulating him. Quickly, she took off the hoodie and stashed it in her bag. Then she checked her makeup in the mirror and brushed her hair until it shone against her black crop top. She pulled off her sneakers, stashed them in the bag, and put on her new shoes.

A bit dressed up for a high school basketball game, possibly, but not at all for getting a man back.

"Bye. See you at the next game." The eyes of number twenty-five's mother widened. "Wow. You look—nice." The last word lifted in a question, which Anya did not intend to answer.

"Thank you," she said and turned away.

Anya followed the people who had been sitting in front of her as they stepped down from the bleachers, one by one. Her plan was to get down to the floor and step out from behind the celebrating crowd at just the right time, when the others had left, to greet Ryder. That way, she wouldn't have to stand around awkwardly waiting, but there would still be enough people in the vicinity so he couldn't choose to totally ignore her.

At least she hoped that was the way it would work.

The first step down told her she should have waited to change into the heels. The next step, when she wobbled even more dangerously, confirmed it, and by the third step, she was pretty sure the only thing that stood between her and the excruciating embarrassment of a broken leg was the common sense to remove the shoes.

A minor adjustment to the plan. Nothing catastrophic.

Still shielded by the people in front of her, she reached down to pull off her right shoe at the same time the smallest child of the extra-tall family decided to shriek her protest over being told to finish her drink before she got to the car. She yanked her hand from her mother's, her small features indignant, and the liquid in her drink went flying through the air straight back toward Anya, who was so focused on avoiding it, she leaned to the left and lost her balance, which she hadn't secured in the first place.

The orange pop found her anyway, landing in her hair and on her crop top, while the child froze midscream and her mother turned in horror, pulling the child close. "I'm sorry, so sorry," Anya heard the mom say from above her as she went tumbling, head over high heels, to the next wooden bleacher down and then the next, people scrambling to get out of her way. Then one heel lodged in the wooden slat beneath the seat, stopping her descent.

Ow. Ow. And really, *ow.*

Arms reached toward her, along with several questions from several people. "Are you all right?" "Is she okay?" "What happened?" and "Did you see *that?*"

She wasn't all right. Her shoulder hurt, her knee hurt, her hair and top were a mess, and as for her pride, it was pretty much in shambles. "I'm fine," she insisted. "Please. I'm fine."

The child looked frightened, standing perfectly still as the remains of orange pop dripped down the tiny fingers that clutched the cup. "I've told you and told you," said her mom, jerking on her free hand. "See what happens when you have a tantrum? Look what you've done to that lady."

If the little girl's expression was any indication, Anya decided, she must look way past terrible. "It's okay. Not her fault. I wasn't looking where I was going."

She accepted a hand up from a determined dad-person, whose small son watched Anya, his open mouth forming an "o." The heel of one shoe was lodged in a wooden slat, so she stood lopsided, but tried to make it look deliberate as she waved people to move on. "I'm good. Thank you." Her knee really did hurt. A lot.

"You should have somebody take a look at you."

Not a chance. "I will. Thanks."

When they did leave, reluctantly and still looking over their shoulders at her, she furiously worked to pull the heel out of its trap. It wouldn't budge. Frustrated, she grabbed the shoe with both hands, ignoring her protesting shoulder and knee, and yanked. Hard.

So hard that, when the heel broke off, she fell back, her buttocks landing on the wood above so that she straddled the seat. The heel clattered to the floor.

She looked up, still in disbelief at how one simple plan could go so wrong, to see Ryder directly in front of her on the floor, only two rows down. He hesitated a beat and then held up his hands, palms out, displaying a five with one hand, a four with the other.

His eyes held hers. He lifted an eyebrow and said, "I would give you a ten for style alone, but have to deduct a point for loss of equipment."

Anya's mouth opened. And closed, without saying a word.

"Okay, fine," he said, lowering his hands. "Nine point five, because maybe the equipment was defective, but that's as far as I'm going to go."

Just the sight of him up close mesmerized her. When she watched him from afar, he was gorgeous, with his rumpled dark hair, determined chin, and broad smile. But when he was looking right at her, from this close, with that clear, steady gaze of eyes so dark brown she could melt in them, her heartbeat skittered.

Anya's breath caught and held.

Once again, dizziness came over her without warning, yet another video clip playing in her mind. This time, it was of Ryder, his hair long and unkempt, a steely bitterness in his eyes that drove straight through her. The image flickered, disappeared, reappeared again.

She blinked and it was gone, leaving her to realize that it was a very different Ryder in front of her.

As she lay sprawled across the bleachers. Sticky, bumped, bruised, and one-shoed.

CHAPTER SIX

Ryder stared at the woman he had loved more than anything in the world, before and after he'd had to let her go.

He hadn't seen Anya since that time in rehab when he'd shut her out, done everything possible, without using words, to make her feel unwelcome. He hadn't wanted her to come back, hadn't wanted to face her.

The whole fucking accident had been his fault. He'd been the one who'd gotten so trashed he couldn't drive, who had let that girl crawl all over him until Anya had seen red.

Shit, he'd been such an immature jerk back then. Reveling in the attention a basketball star gets and thinking he had it all, so he could take more.

Yeah, look what all of that had got him. He still loved the strategy of the game, as well as the teamwork and the discipline it demanded, but he didn't like what all the accolades could do to kids who let it get to them. So he didn't allow that with the kids he coached.

Good thing he'd grown up, at least some, since rehab. No, scratch that. He'd just been able to claim better control of his emotions where she was concerned, learned how to put on a good face. That probably didn't count as growing up.

He kept his gaze even, steady, unfazed, though his heart hammered out of his chest.

"Coach?" he heard one of his players ask. "You okay?"

"I'm good," he said automatically, without taking his eyes off Anya. She got up slowly, with her crazy-ass shoes, one missing a heel, in her hands. She looked embarrassed. She looked more beautiful than ever. Her top was spattered with something liquid that made the fabric cling to her breasts, and her hair stuck out on one side.

He remembered the feel of her breasts in his hands. It took a rapid intake of breath and a *no fucking way* message to his brain to make the memory disappear. Which it did. Temporarily.

One side of her face had orange on it. Now he got it. She'd met up with orange pop. And lost.

He couldn't help it; his gaze darted to her left hand. No ring.

"So. Anya," he said, attempting casual, nonchalant. His hands gripped the wheels of his chair, as ready to flee as he was ready to stay rooted to this spot. "It's been a long time." He flinched inside as he said it. All this time, and that's the best he could come up with?

From behind, one of his players bumped his shoulder. "Sorry, Coach."

"Hit the showers, guys," he called. "I'll see you in a few minutes."

They obeyed, their teenage feet pounding on the wooden floor, leaping toward the basket, unable to contain their excited yells. Tinsel from a cheerleader's pom-pom skittered through the air to land on his leg. He brushed it away.

"It has been a long time," Anya finally answered, agony playing out on her face.

"What are you doing?"

"There was a kid in front of me who didn't want to leave without her drink and she got upset with her mom and the next thing I knew, the whole thing went flying and landed on me." She looked down and then put a hand on her hip, apparently hoping to appear as casual about this whole thing as he hoped he did. "Then I sort of lost my footing and went down, but it's no big thing."

He wanted to laugh, but he spotted a glimmer of tears in the corner of her eyes and knew he couldn't. "I meant, what are you doing here, at the game?"

A hand through her hair. An apparently sticky hand, since it caught on the few strands that didn't already look as though they'd gone through a food processor. She stared at her hand and then wiped it on her jeans. It took two tries to free her fingers from the denim. "I heard the team is good. And you're coaching. I just, you know, wanted to see for myself."

She shifted her weight from one hip to the other, awkwardly, self-consciously. "You're the coach," she repeated.

"So they tell me." He kept his expression purposely unreadable, a skill that came in handy at times. Like this time.

But inside, his emotions were running all over the place, sprinting, rebounding, taking dunk shots, until they so overwhelmed him, he wanted to be anywhere but here. Even he knew, though, that there was only one way out of this. With a flick of his wrists, he rolled the chair to the edge of the bleachers, pulling to a stop. He extended his hand.

"I'm a mess," she said.

"You never could put one foot in front of the other without getting tangled up," he teased.

She hesitated and then stepped down from the bleachers in her bare feet, taking his hand as she came to the last one, the step to the floor. As their hands touched, an ache of longing went through him. He clenched his jaw and rolled back slowly, helping her down to the floor. Just as he would anyone else.

Except that she wasn't anyone else. Never had been and never would be. At one time, she'd known his deepest thoughts and craziest dreams, the ones he'd never told to anyone else.

She held on to his hand a second longer than necessary, but then pulled it away, leaving him with something sticky on his skin. He decided to ignore it.

Her expression relaxed. It took a few seconds, but the corners of her mouth turned up in a tentative smile. "*Me?* You're the one who did a slam dunk in that big game against Gonzaga and fell on your butt, all in the same move." Then just as quickly as her features had smoothed, they contorted in anxiety again. "I didn't mean—I shouldn't have—"

"Relax." He raised his hand, waving away her concern. "You're right. I did. And I think it still hurts." He indicated his backside.

"It does?"

He shook his head. "Kidding. Only my pride hurts over that one." Fuck, he had to get better at reading people. At knowing when he could joke about his situation and when he couldn't.

He'd once been able to read Anya better than anyone in the whole world. So much for that.

"So, anyway. You coached great," she said with a shade too much enthusiasm. Her lower lip quivered. "Congratulations."

"Thanks." Most of the crowd had emptied out of the gym, but there were still a few people left. Hands patted him on the back, with murmurs of, "Great game, Coach," and, "See you next week." He acknowledged them with nods and smiles and then, his expression again impassive, turned back to Anya. "How are you?"

Three words. People said them every day, but he really, *really* wanted to know the answer. And he didn't want her to see how much he wanted to know.

"Fine. Just working. You know…" her voice trailed off and her hand flailed helplessly, as though trying to find a gesture she couldn't locate.

He tipped his head, studying her. "I hear you have a new job you like."

She nodded hard, overdoing it by a mile. "With Zest. It's a fashion retailer. And magazine. You probably don't—"

"I do. I've seen Zest. Some good men's stuff."

"Oh." Her gaze shifted to his chair and then back to his eyes, her cheeks pinking. "Of course."

He couldn't resist. "You wear clothes whether you can walk or not. In fact, it's pretty much recommended. At least when you're in public."

Her cheeks flamed. He'd gone too far. Regret stabbed through him. "Sorry. Meant it as a joke." Another one that had fallen flat. He looked away, back toward the gym's exit door. Who the hell was he kidding; she'd never *not* be uncomfortable around him. Too much history. Too many mistakes.

A laugh, only halfway, but an attempt. "Good one."

His gaze met hers again. "I'd better go." He jabbed his thumb back over his shoulder, in the direction of the locker room. *Tell me not to. Or say you'll wait until I come back.*

Instead, she picked up her bag and said, "Me, too. Anyway, congratulations again. It always feels good to beat a rival team."

Right. Good thing she hadn't said what he'd thought he wanted to hear. They were both better off that way, since his heart was now doing this weird thumping thing and his brain was skittering around his memory to pull up all sorts of images of him and Anya. *Before.*

"Thanks," he said, hands on the wheels. "Good seeing you." He didn't wait for her to answer before rolling away, and he didn't have to look back to know she was watching him. His fist clenched to pound the door leading to the locker room open, as though the resulting pain in his hand could somehow overtake and relieve the one in his heart.

Didn't work. Of course it fucking didn't.

* * *

Watching him, Anya sucked in a breath and didn't let it out until he'd gone through doors that badly needed a new paint job. How could she? How could she have reminded him of a time when his legs worked? How could she have made him feel different from every other man who bought clothes?

All she'd wanted to do was tell him how much she missed him. How good he looked. How she wished, so badly, they could find a way to start over again, to see if it could work this time, now that they were older, smarter.

Annie Sterling never would have had this kind of trouble. She would have successfully ducked that kid's flying pop and high-stepped her way down the bleachers in heels without missing a beat. Ryder would have fallen all over himself to get her to stay. That was how cool Annie was. And how not-cool Anya was.

Anya walked slowly toward the gym's exit door, her head and heart heavy, her shoes in her hand, and her feet making lonely sticky suction noises on the floor.

Damn Annie Sterling, anyway. The bitch could do it all.

CHAPTER SEVEN

"You did *what?*" Anya's friend Caitlin was incredulous. "Why didn't you just watch the game on TV, like a normal person?"

"It's high school. It probably wasn't on TV and even if it had been, the camera would have been on the players, not on the coach. And that's who I wanted to see." Anya stirred her vodka tonic with her index finger, feeling self-conscious at Caitlin's reaction. "It made sense at the time."

"No, it didn't."

Caitlin had little-to-no filter. Where most people would make sympathetic listening noises and think their own private thoughts, Caitlin called bullshit. Every time. It was one of her most irritating and endearing qualities.

"Doesn't matter now," Anya said. "I got my answer."

"No. You *didn't.*"

Anya exhaled in exasperation, something she knew Caitlin was used to. "He still wants nothing to do with me. Was only polite because I looked like an idiot sprawled across the bleachers with orange pop all over me and a broken shoe."

Cait's brows drew together as she pondered this. "Maybe."

"I've showered twice, but I still smell like sweat socks and dust. I swear, it crawled out of the walls and glued itself to me."

Her friend leaned in, her perfect nose taking a delicate sniff. "You smell like soap."

"So what do I do now? I should leave it alone, right?" Anya drew an invisible circle on the table with her vodka finger. "But I can't. I want to see him. I keep thinking that if I just had a chance to really talk with him…"

"He'd magically forgive you and everything would be as it was before?"

"Could be." She had the feeling this was a trick question.

"Except that he can't walk and you can't forget he can't walk."

It *had* been a trick question. Why was she friends with Caitlin, again? Oh. Because Caitlin had come up to her at Zest one day to announce she'd decided they were going to be friends, and Anya, who didn't know Caitlin at that time, had gone along with it.

"Leaving me stuck with the Zekes of the world."

"Because that's the kind of guy you go for now."

Anger pulled at Anya. It wasn't as though Caitlin had any sort of perfect track record with men. The last one—oh, wait. He'd wanted to marry her, like most of the others. Just the latest in a string of husband applicants Caitlin had judged vaguely imperfect for her tastes.

Judged. Caitlin did *that* part perfectly. Anya's indignation reached full boil, hissing and steaming as it spilled over. This friendship had to be reaching its expiration date, no matter what Caitlin said. "Listen, Caitlin," she bit out before stopping short, her attention caught by a flash of orange hair. At the back of the bar. On the head of a woman. A woman who was now hiding said head under a table.

Orange hair. Poof.

Dizziness again. She very possibly had a brain tumor. Or she was going crazy. Or—Anya pressed a hand to her forehead. Pictures flashed before her eyes. Ryder. Herself. The accident. She shivered, which made her even more woozy.

"What's wrong?" Caitlin asked, leaning forward.

"That woman over there. I know her. Somehow, I know her."

Caitlin turned and dipped her chin, trying to see beneath the tablecloth. "And she's trying to hide from you?"

Anya frowned. Then she smoothed her forehead and tried closing her eyes. One word—poof—kept rolling through her mind, over and over, until she wanted to scream to make it stop.

"There's only one way to find out how you know her," she heard Caitlin say.

Anya's eyes flew open. "Wait. *No.*" She didn't know why, but she didn't think she wanted to know the answer.

Too late. Caitlin was already striding toward the orange-haired woman, who was alone at her table. And still under the tablecloth.

Dread filled Anya as she watched Caitlin, feet spread, hands on her hips. When her friend wanted to know something, there was no stopping her. Grown men had been known to scatter in alarm.

New images began flashing through her mind. Her face, with an ugly scar on the cheek. Ryder at the rehab center, his features twisted in a mixture of what looked like pain and grief. A water bottle he heaved toward her that bounced off the wall. Anya's mother, shaking her head, with a death hold on soggy tissues she kept using to dab at her eyes. Ryder shouting at Anya, telling her he wished he'd never met her and to go away and leave him alone.

And she had. God help her, she had. When she never, ever should have. Anya's stomach turned over. She clutched at it, to no avail. This couldn't be true. Her hand slid upward to feel her cheek, the skin smooth beneath her touch. No scar.

Then Cait was standing before her, with the woman in tow. The orange hair was even more jarring at this range, despite the bar's dim lighting, or possibly because the skin next to it was so white, with its fine scattering of wrinkles, and dark lipstick. Several gold necklaces around her neck appeared to be pulling her head forward.

Her eyes were wide, startled.

Caitlin could, and often did, have that effect on people.

"She says her name is Claire and you've done business together."

"*Madame* Claire," Anya said, surprising herself. She looked around to see if that had come from someone else. It hadn't.

"Indeed," the woman agreed. She had an accent that not only sounded familiar, but also made the hairs at the back of Anya's neck stand on end. "Now I must go."

"You're not going anywhere," Caitlin pronounced. "You're going to talk to my friend while I go check out that guy at the bar. I'll be back in a few minutes, so say whatever it is you have to say."

Anya attempted a protest that never made it out of her mouth. She didn't know who this woman was, except that she *did*, but never mind that. Either way, she didn't want anything to do with her. As Caitlin stepped back to leave, Anya felt desperate to grab her arm and make her stay.

Something she didn't want to think about was associated with this woman, this Claire. Claire didn't look happy, either, but she sat down, glaring at Caitlin's retreating back. She turned her attention to Anya. "Do you remember me?" she asked, her voice quavering on the last word, as though she was worried about the answer. Her face pinched tight.

"No," Anya whispered, even as she nodded her head *yes*. "I don't think so."

"Nothing?"

Yes, something. "No."

The other woman's features relaxed.

"Good. And you are happy."

None of her business. Anya sat back against the leather booth and studied the woman. She lifted a shoulder. "I guess."

"We are done, then."

Done. Everyone was done with her lately, it seemed. "What do you care if I'm happy or not?" Anya blurted. Where the hell had that come from? Of course she was happy. Sort of. And how rude to say that to a stranger. Her mother would be appalled. She tried desperately to find her apology smile, the one that always made everything right.

That smile, once so useful, had been missing in action since she'd seen Ryder. And it had apparently decided it wasn't showing up now.

Claire's mouth opened and closed. After a minute, she said, "If you are not happy, that is only your choice to make. Does not concern me." She didn't sound convinced; she sounded nervous.

"I don't know why *anything* about me would concern you." God, her head hurt. A stabbing pain that demanded attention she didn't want to give. Probably the tumor growing bigger. "Tell me how we supposedly know each other."

"It is of no consequence," the woman said briskly. "I will go now."

As she put a hand on table to push away, Anya said, "Poof. What does that mean? Why can't I get it out of my head?"

Claire looked startled. "I am sure I would not know," she mumbled, eyes fixed on the table. She began to rise from the chair.

"You do know." She didn't understand a lot, but she was sure of that.

The woman stood.

Time to summon her inner Caitlin. "Sit. *Down.*" Not as authoritative, but not bad.

The other woman's mouth pickled, but she did as she was told.

"Explain it to me."

"I am sure there is not anything to say."

"Tell. Me."

"Not a good idea."

"Tell—"

"As you wish." The woman's voice was high, impatient. She shook her head and heaved a sigh so large, the necklaces around her neck rattled. "You recall nothing?" Claire's fingers tapped the table, in a relentless thump, thump.

"About what?" Anya shook her head. Slivers of dread snaked her spine.

"The wedding. Of your cousin."

And then suddenly, Anya did remember, with a force that rocked her head back against the booth. This woman had…had…given Anya a…do-over. *Fuck, fuck, fuck. What the fuck had it been? And who the hell gets a do-over, for anything?*

"Because you should not. And there is no reason that you must." The woman's words ran together, spilling across the table to fling cold drops of memory onto Anya's face. Madame Claire looked beyond nervous now. She looked ready to bolt from the table.

"I remember. Omigod, I do." This wasn't happening. She glanced at Caitlin, still at the bar. At the cute guy still flirting with Caitlin, at the wooden floor, scuffed but gleaming, at the table, at the— *Shit.* "You did some kind of a spell." It was coming back to her now. "You were supposed to have erased the accident, kept it from happening." Her breath came fast, her chest rising and falling.

She remembered her one request, the shaky hope that had consumed her at the idea it could even actually happen. The woman's assurances that she could do it this once, just once. No one else could do it, only her. Poof. Just like that, the accident would be gone. Erased. Would never have happened.

Anya's biggest mistake. This woman had promised to make it disappear. But it was still fucking here.

Madame Claire's fingers quit their tapping. "I must go," she murmured.

"The hell you must." Anya slapped her hand on top of the older woman's, holding it fast against the table. "You're not going anywhere until I know what's going on. Why the spell didn't work. You said it would."

"Really, it is not what you think—"

"I think he's still paralyzed. I *know* he's still paralyzed." Her voice rose, in fear, in anger. From the corner of her eye, she saw Caitlin glance over from her seat at the bar. Anya lowered her voice, but venom still wove through it. "You *promised* me you could do this. Make it so the accident never happened."

The penciled eyebrows bobbed up and down like a crazed caterpillar. "I did do this. But possibly—it may be that something was left out. Here or there. Yes, possibly, there." The last word sounded like a squeak.

"Left out? Are you serious?"

"Not that I could know, of course." The psychic smoothed her orange hair and shrunk back in the chair. "I did not. Know."

"You didn't know, but you're here. And you were watching me. So you at least suspected."

"I wanted to find out. That all was well."

Anya didn't buy the casual tone. "You wanted to see what kind of a mess you'd made?" Oh God, oh God…the accident had still happened; only now, Anya, who had been responsible for it, had come out of it without a scratch.

The guilt hit her so hard, she bent forward, clutching her stomach. "I can't believe this," she said to the table. "She promised me. She said it would all be all right, that the accident would never have happened."

Before…*Before* there had been consequences for her, too. The scar.

"The pancakes. Blueberry. I could not think; I was so distracted. You did not taste them, I'm thinking. You ran away too fast." Madame Claire raised her chin. "Very good pancakes."

Anya lifted her head to stare. "You can't be serious. You screwed up my life because of blueberry pancakes."

"The smell." The psychic fluttered her fingers in front of her nose. "As I said, so good. But it is a shame, is it not, that the spell, it did not work. And perhaps you will have these moments when you remember from both. An unfortunate thing, that, but it cannot be helped now."

"Both."

"Yes, you know." The psychic looked at her as though she were dense. "Your life before. And after." She dropped her voice. "These flashes may come like a lightbulb that does not work, is not…" She appeared to search for a word, finally landing on one. "Tight in its socket." She shook her head. "I talked with my mother. Nothing to be done for it now, but should go away as you settle into the after. So that is it. Be happy now and all will be well."

Anya rose from the table, her fingers clenched in a strangle move as a guttural sound came from her mouth.

Madame Claire drew back in horror, kicking at another chair, which hit the floor with a bang. She backpedaled on the floor, hands in front of her, urging no action. Next thing Anya knew, Caitlin was at her side, grabbing her hands to lower them. "What the hell is going on?" Caitlin demanded.

"This woman ruined my life," Anya snarled. "Ruined *Ryder's* life. His one chance."

"Is not true. You no longer have the scar. Your life, it is fine." Madame Claire's eyes were wide. "The man, I am sorry. There was, yes, a problem. But your life, you have what you want, do you not?"

"No. I do not." Anya couldn't breathe, couldn't think. And her wrists stung where Caitlin held them fast.

"What's she talking about?" Caitlin asked. "What scar?"

"Put it back," Anya ordered, trying to climb past Caitlin to get to the psychic. "Put it all back, the scar. Everything." *Ryder.* She physically hurt at the thought he'd been so close to escaping injury.

Madame Claire shook her head. "That I cannot do. It is too dangerous."

"Is somebody going to tell me what's going on? I hate to point this out, but we're becoming the entertainment here."

Caitlin was right, Anya realized. People were staring, beginning to gather around them. One of them was a manager type, who was pushing his way through. He looked upset.

Frustration, sadness, and anger rippled through her until her entire body shook. She wanted to say so much, but couldn't make a single word come out.

Caitlin took charge. "You," she pointed at the psychic. "Get out of here. And *you*," she pointed this time at Anya, whose one hand she still held, "come with me. We're getting out of here, too."

Anya let herself be led away. She didn't say a word as Caitlin drove her back to her apartment, instead staring out of the car window while she tried to reconcile the memories, the images in her mind with what had happened *before* and *after*. They refused to neatly sort into mental filing cabinets.

"So you're not going to tell me what's going on," Caitlin tried again, gripping the steering wheel hard. "I liked that guy at the bar, you know. So I figure you owe me. We had to leave before I could give him my number."

"Doesn't matter. He'll find you." They always did, where Cait was concerned.

"Thanks for the confidence." Sarcasm dripped from Cait's words.

They rode in silence again for several minutes before Cait asked, "That woman, should I have let you take her on? If I had, would she have made it out of the place alive?"

"Yes. And probably not."

Cait tipped her head. "For someone who won't even kill a spider, that says a lot. What did she do?"

"I can't tell you." Only a few minutes ago, she'd remembered a warning from the psychic, spoken over blueberry pancakes. If Anya told anyone, *all could unravel most unpredictably.* As if it hadn't already. "I would if I could, but I can't."

Caitlin nodded. "Okay, then." She pulled the car to a stop in front of Anya's building. "Is there anything I can do to help?"

Redo my do-over. Talk me out of ever going to a psychic in the first place. "No. But thank you." She gave her friend the best imitation of a smile she could manage and climbed out of the car.

"Hey," Caitlin called after her. "Why don't you go play Annie Sterling for a while? Might make you feel better."

"You could be right." Anya shut the door and walked away, hating do-overs, Annie, orange hair, psychics, *and* bars in general.

Settle into her life "after." As if.

CHAPTER EIGHT

Bo bounded up with a hug the minute Anya walked through the apartment door. She buried her face in his soft golden coat, rattling the license tags on his collar and inhaling his familiar doggie smell, a mixture of the lavender shampoo she'd used on him last night and an aroma he'd acquired just by being a dog.

After a few minutes of nonjudgmental, unbridled love from her dog, she felt better, calmer. As though she might be able to make baby steps into the world again.

She stroked his ears, loving their softness between her fingers. "How are you doing, big guy?"

Bo ruffed an answer and aimed a meaningful look at his jar of treats, waiting on the counter.

"You'll get one when you've done your business. You know that." She grabbed his leather leash and fastened it to his collar. "C'mon, let's go, cookie monster. You need to go out and I need to clear my head."

A walk through the sweet, crisp air helped. With every step on the pavement, she forced herself to put more pieces of the "before" memory together. She, and not her parents, had gone to Chase's wedding. She remembered how beautiful it had been, how much love had been in the air, and how it had all depressed her, no matter how hard she'd tried to be upbeat.

The fingers of her free hand reached up to touch her left cheek. It had been right there, the scar. People had looked, people had wondered. And she'd learned how to hide it when she needed to or put it on full display when that served a purpose.

Now that she'd granted permission, the memories came flooding back so vividly, she had to put up a virtual stop sign in her brain, instructing each to wait its turn until she could process them. The psychic with her arms raised, the small-town diner with peeling plastic on its benches, the fluffy blueberry pancakes that made her mouth water thinking about them now.

But the spell hadn't worked. And things were much worse because of it. She'd rather live with the scar than with the additional guilt of knowing she'd come out of the accident unscathed. No wonder Ryder had looked at her like that. He had to have wondered why she would show up to flaunt her lack of injuries, even as he dealt with his.

And like an idiot, she'd fallen all over herself in front of him, even though *she* could walk perfectly fine.

Bo pulled to a halt at a tree and Anya followed suit. She leaned against the bark for support and a twig pushed at her thin top, sharp and insistent. "Good boy," she said once he had done his business, her mind only half engaged in the present.

Bo looked up at her, a question in his eyes. She patted his head absently. "Yes, we're going home now."

The thing was, Ryder hadn't looked as though he couldn't stand the sight of her when they'd seen each other at the game the other night. And she'd been pretty much at her all-time worst, appearance-wise, a fact confirmed by the mirror at home. Orange pop didn't mix well with mascara and eyeliner.

In fact, she'd seen a flicker of something in Ryder's expression that had given her brief hope. At least until his face had shut down any unauthorized transmissions.

She had to know how he felt about her now. Whether he was bitter, whether he hated her. Whether he was only being polite when he hadn't ordered her out of the gym he now called home. A coach probably had to be nice to community members, by contract.

Whether that flicker of something more had been there, or she'd imagined it.

So she'd find out. Through the one person she knew he would talk to. She increased the speed of her steps and jangled the leash, urging Bo to do the same. He happily trotted at the new pace to the end of one block and then the next. Once inside her apartment, she released her dog from his leash, gave him his treat, and pulled off her coat, heading straight for her laptop.

She'd meant to drop the coat on the chair, but it missed, landing on the floor. Didn't matter. She had more pressing things on her mind.

Just because she wrote a message didn't mean she had to send it. She could, and was ninety-nine percent sure she would, delete it without sending. But now that it was in her head, it wouldn't leave.

She began a text to Ryder. *You've never said why you're in a wheelchair. What happened, do you feel comfortable sharing?* No. Sounded like a psychologist. She backspaced to clear the words. *So,*

I'm just wondering, not that it matters, but—Wrong. No buts. She stared at the phone, hoping for wisdom. She could ask Suri what to say, but, no.

She tried again. *A quick question. You don't have to answer*—

Ping. A message. From Ryder. *Are you trying to send me a text?*

He must have seen those dots that said she was typing. The two of them were so in sync, they were thinking about texting each other at the same time. Just as a warm feeling began to wash over her, she remembered that she didn't know how to phrase what she wanted to know. And those three dots had ratted her out.

Yes, she answered. Her fingers hovered over the keyboard, not sure what to say next. Maybe she could say something else, something not soaked with danger. She thought. And thought some more, but all she could think of was the wrong question.

Because Anya was thinking, instead of Annie, she realized. *Think like Annie.*

What's on your mind? he texted.

She had to reply. With something. After a tense moment, she typed, *I don't know how to ask this.*

How did I get so handsome? He put a smiley face next to it and then answered his own question. *Genetics.*

Anya nodded to herself. Ryder's parents were both very good-looking, in the high-maintenance-but-looks-effortless kind of way. He'd never had to bother with that, though; he looked adorable even when he climbed out of bed in the morning. *Bed. With Ryder.* She flashed back and had to catch her breath at the memory.

How did I get to be such a great dog dad?

He was a great dog dad. And still she couldn't type out the question.

I was raised by two dogs. They trained me right.

Despite the butterflies leaping in her stomach, she grinned and glanced over at Bo. He cocked his head to one side in a question. "I know," she said to him. "I'm trying." She had just put her finger on the key to start typing when his next text came through. *How did I end up in a wheelchair?*

Anya squeezed her eyes shut, then opened them and answered, *How did you?*

She held her breath until she saw his answer. *I could say it was dumb luck, but really, it was a car accident. In college.*

What now? Anya would say she was sorry. What would Annie say? Annie was more like Caitlin. *What happened?*

Hit another car. Got hurt. That's pretty much it.

No it wasn't. Not by a long shot. She held her breath again. *The other car's fault?*

A mistake. That's why they call it an accident.

He wasn't blaming her. He wasn't. *That's a pretty big mistake. How do you feel about it?*

Like it doesn't do any good to think about it. Things happen. It is what it is and if you keep going over the past, you get stuck there.

Shit, he'd come a long way, while she was—well, at least she was trying to get over what had happened. In her own way. She couldn't let this go, yet. *Was anyone else with you?* She briefly closed her eyes, waiting for his reply, attempting to telepathically signal him that he could be honest, tell her…or Annie…exactly how he felt.

But their telepathic towers had been shut down for several years. Now the dots were on his side. She waited. Then came his reply. *My girlfriend, at the time.*

Was she hurt, too? The correct answer was that she'd suffered a mortal wound to the heart. Not that she expected Ryder to respond with that.

No.

A statement of fact that didn't tell her anything. Was he really that over what had happened? She wasn't buying it.

His next message changed the subject. *I'm making a trip over the President's Day break. To New York. I want to meet you. Enough with online.*

Shit, shit. Double shit. She couldn't do this. He couldn't meet Annie, who, after all, didn't exist. Rapid-fire, she texted, *Oh no! I want to meet you in person more than anything, but I'm going to be gone over President's Day break. Going to my sister's in*—she paused, fingers above the keys, then resumed—*Canada. She has six kids, is pregnant again, and moving to a new house. I have to help.*

There. That would end that. No one in his right mind would want to accompany her to Canada to help a pregnant woman with six kids move. Not even Ryder. She shook her head in wonder. Amazing how the lies just tripped right off her fingers. She should probably be worried about that.

It took a minute for his reply to appear. *Works out fine because your break is the week before mine. Remember?*

Oh hell. Now she did. She'd been so proud of herself for doing her Internet homework on the small town where she'd decided Annie would live, she'd mentioned to him that the school district there didn't do a President's Day break; they did a Winter Break, instead. And she'd told him what week that was.

You're right! It does work out fine. Thank God he couldn't see her face. Thank God she couldn't see her own face right now, which she could feel burning hot with anxiety. She'd created Annie, now she'd have to deliver her.

Good thing her mother had no knowledge of this mess. Anya could practically hear her reciting, in her most annoying sing-song voice, "Oh what a tangled web we weave…" Not fair, especially because it was true.

Another text from him. *Let's plan on it.*

Absolutely. Can't wait. God help her.

Me, neither. Gotta go. Early practice tomorrow. So when I come out, you'll take me to that caramel place you're always talking about?

Anya loved caramel, more than any other food. To her, it was a food group all on its own. When she'd been deciding on Annie's fictional town, she'd discovered that Castle Falls, New York, was the self-proclaimed caramel capital of the world. That was all she'd needed to land Annie there. *Be prepared to get sticky, Ryder Brandt.*

Sounds intriguing…

You don't know the half of it. If only Anya did.

Your sister going to be able to get moved? Do I need to arrange to help?

He was a good guy, such a good guy. Zeke would have already had a reason he couldn't possibly help. Back problems, a broken shoelace. Whatever. *She'll be fine. Thanks.*

Three weeks 'til break. Not sure I can wait that long. 'Night.

'Night.

Anya dropped the phone to the bed and flopped back, arm above her head, to stare at the ceiling. She'd just set up the one man she'd ever truly and thoroughly loved, and couldn't bear to hurt more than she already had, with another woman. A woman who didn't exist.

What the hell was she doing to do?

Even Caitlin would have trouble getting out of this one.

CHAPTER NINE

By the time Anya woke in the morning, she had an earring indentation behind her ear and a lace pattern on her stomach from falling asleep fully clothed, but she had the beginnings of a plan.

A rough plan, granted, and likely fraught with peril, but a plan, nonetheless. And a backup plan, in case the first one didn't work. Which it probably wouldn't. And a backup to the backup, in case...well, neither one worked.

She was going to get Ryder to fall for Anya again, and forget all about Annie. This do-over, however wrong it had turned out, was going to fly.

Clarity and determination put new purpose into her morning walk with Bo. The dog turned to look back at her a couple of times, as if to ask when their casual stroll had turned into a march. She bobbed her head at him. *Get used to it, mister.*

She dressed, made and ate her toast, and brushed her teeth with similar precision. No more falling down bleachers. No more meltdowns because of strange women with orange hair. Anya Ramsey was in charge of her own life and do-over. Maybe for the first time, but not for the last.

On the drive to work, she listened to NPR's *Morning Edition*. More serious, grown-up than her usual station. She shook her head at the story on where Ebola might emerge next and listened with interest to the story of an eighty-five-year-old Turkish fashionista who had immigrated to Germany.

When she arrived at the company's building, she pulled her car into a parking spot, shut it off, and walked briskly to the door. Anyone who saw her would say, *That woman has everything together*, she decided. *Knows what she wants and how to get it. Probably even listens to NPR instead of morning radio junk.*

Well, yes, she did.

Once she'd had her coffee and checked her desk, Anya squared her shoulders and readied herself to put the first part of the plan in motion. Good thing her supervisor, Mollie, liked her. Trading in on some of that good cred could go a long way.

"Hey," she said, knocking lightly on the open door to Mollie's office.

The other woman looked up. "Hey. How are you this morning, Anya?"

"Great. Thanks. Really, you know, great."

Mollie nodded, her eyebrows raised expectantly.

"You said to come with you with ideas and I have one." She sucked in a breath. Some of that NPR-high was beginning to fade.

"Great." Mollie sat back in her chair, pen in her hand. "Let's hear it."

"For menswear. I have this—this *friend*. Who is very good-looking. Model good-looking."

"Oh." Her supervisor now looked less enthused. "That could describe a lot of people."

Not necessarily. Besides, Ryder was better than model good-looking. He was real person good-looking. "True. But he's different. He uses a wheelchair."

Mollie's eyebrows drew together. She was paying closer attention now. "Really."

"And he's my age, a great dresser, very familiar with menswear, how to look good. I was thinking…" Another deep breath.

She didn't have to finish the sentence. Mollie did it for her. "You were thinking we might be able to use him in some ads."

"Yes."

"Interesting." Mollie tapped the pen against her chin, unwittingly leaving a spot of blue ink on her skin. "I might like it."

Anya waited, not daring to get her hopes up and trying not to stare at Mollie's ink-stained chin.

"Do you have a photo of him?"

"Just one. I printed it from his Facebook page." She reached into her pocket to pull it out and walked toward Mollie's desk. She extended the picture toward her supervisor. No one had to know about the photo of Ryder from ten years ago, before the accident. The one she still kept tucked in her wallet, though it was now frayed around the edges and the color had faded.

Mollie took it, looking closely. "Interesting," she said again. "He is a good-looking guy. And he's into sports?" Ryder was holding a basketball in the photo.

"High school basketball coach and teacher. His kids love him."

"Good body?"

"Oh, *hell* yes," Anya replied before she thought about it. "I mean, yes. He does. Have one. A body."

Mollie continued to examine Ryder's photo. "And he'd like to model?"

"Well, he hasn't said that, in so many words. But I know he would, if he had the chance, and he'd be so great. And different. I mean, you don't have to walk to want to wear clothes you look and feel good in. He'd be perfect for a shoot." *Say yes; say yes.*

Mollie chewed on her lip, managing to transfer dark pink lipstick to her teeth. By the end of the day, Mollie usually wore a few different colors, none of them having to do with her clothing. "We do have a new line we're going to be promoting. Federico Shampas is doing a menswear collection."

"I heard that." *Which gave me the idea.*

Mollie laid the photo on the desk and folded her hands beneath her chin, apparently having come to a decision. "So if you think your friend would be up for it, have him come in for a test shoot."

"I will!" *Too excited. Take it down a notch.* "I mean, I'll find out. I'll talk with him and see if he would like to come in and do that. Because I'm pretty sure he would." She actually had no idea.

"What's his name?"

"Ryder."

Mollie nodded her head. "Okay. Keep me posted." She turned back to the paperwork on her desk, unaware of the ink and lipstick transgressions.

"Definitely. Thanks, Mollie." Anya hesitated. "Oh, you might want to—"

Mollie looked up. "Yes?"

"Just, you know…" Anya circled her mouth with her index finger. "Check a mirror really quick. Nothing wrong," she rushed to say. "But I think your pen might be leaking."

"My pen?" Mollie yanked a desk drawer open, pulling out a pocket mirror.

"And your lipstick."

"My lipstick is leaking?" She opened her mouth. "Oh God, it is," she said rubbing at her teeth. "Thanks."

"Sure." Anya turned to leave.

"Oh, one more thing."

Anya turned back.

"Let's have you do the test shots with him. You can help him." There was a question in Mollie's half smile. "Seeing as he's your friend and all."

Anya felt heat climb to her cheeks. "Thanks. And don't worry, he is just a friend," she said. He wasn't exactly even a friend at this point. But if her plan worked, all of that would change.

It seemed so simple and straightforward.

That was the worrisome part.

* * *

Part two of her plan: Get Ryder on board with being a model. That afternoon, Anya left for lunch early to go by the high school, hoping to catch the coach in his office. She hadn't quite worked out what she would say to him, so on the way over in her car she rehearsed possible approaches. "Hey Ryder, I have this great opportunity for you." She shook her head. Too telemarketer.

"Remember how you always wanted to be featured in a magazine?" *Yeck.* He'd wanted to be in *Sports Illustrated,* as a member of a winning team. Not the same thing. Not even close.

"Ummm...I have to do this photo shoot and I need someone to be in it with me..."

No. He had no reason to want to help her. Especially when the request came from out of the blue after all these years.

Anya sighed. She'd have to hope the right words would strike her when she was in front of him. A photo shoot was so perfect. They would have to work together on this. She could touch him, maybe even put her arms around him, without it being weird or awkward. And he couldn't do anything about it because it was for the camera, right?

Until it turned into something more off camera. Which it would, if she had anything to say about it. Their chemistry had been legendary. Their friends had even commented on it, how when the two of them were together in one place, the electric meters went into overdrive.

She pulled into the high school parking lot, passing two different groups of students who gave her car curious, but fleeting, looks. She remembered being their age; it hadn't been that long ago. The topic of conversation was likely who was dating whom, who wanted to date whom, who had just broken up and why, with some conversation thrown in about how unfair a recent test had been.

A part of her longed for the simpler drama of high school. Even though everything had seemed world altering at the time.

She parked the car and walked toward the front entrance of the school. When she pulled the door open, she was prepared this time for the assault of memories. The mingled and competing aromas of floor polish, overcooked vegetables, and lockers that needed to be cleaned. The sight of sturdy, time-worn brick walls and dimly lit hallways without windows. Her own high school had looked and smelled much the same way. It was probably a requirement.

She spotted a glass door to the administration office and opened it. Inside, a sign marked the way to the principal's office. A brown-haired woman with kind eyes and a smudge on her glasses came up to the counter to greet Anya. "Can I help you?"

"Yes. Please. I'm here to see Ryder Brandt."

"Is the coach expecting you?"

The coach. It sounded so formal when this woman said it. "No. I was hoping to catch him in between class and practice. Will just take a few minutes."

"Okay. Let me see where he is." She consulted a schedule behind the counter, one Anya couldn't get a look at, though she leaned forward to try.

The woman looked up, doing a double take when she saw Anya so close. Anya stepped back, shooting her an apology smile.

"You might be in luck. He should be in his office. Probably eating lunch."

Not precisely luck. *Annie* knew when Ryder had a break in his day. That's why Anya had come now. He often texted Annie around this time.

The woman walked to a phone and hit a couple of buttons. "Your name, dear?"

"Anya."

"Pretty name." She nodded and spoke into the receiver.

"Thank you," Anya murmured, hoping Ryder didn't respond by saying he was too busy to see her. Not after she'd come to his school. Not after she'd developed this long-shot plan that probably wouldn't work, but if it did, would be pretty amazing.

The woman returned, somehow managing another smudge on her glasses in that short amount of time. "Okay, all set. Just go out this door," she leaned across the counter to point to the left, "down the first hall to your left and then to office 192. That's where the coaches are."

He'd said he would see her. She resisted the urge to make a happy sound and instead waved her thanks to the woman and set off in the direction she'd indicated. A grown-up. Here on business. Too bad she had to keep reminding herself of that. There was something about a high school, something that lived and breathed in the air, that made her feel seventeen.

Speaking of breathing, she might want to do that again. Hard, though, when she was anticipating seeing Ryder.

The closer she came to office 192, the more her pulse sped up. When at last she peeked around the door, she saw a large common area with small offices opening off of it. A few chairs, a metal table with newspapers scattered on it, and a bank of aging file cabinets filled the open area. She stepped inside, skirted one chair, and zeroed in on the office with the sign that read *Coach Brandt.* The door was closed.

She drew her shoulders up, cleared her throat, and tapped on the wood.

"Come in."

That had to be his teacher/coach voice, commanding and in charge. And sexy. *Really* sexy.

She turned the knob and went inside. Ryder sat at the desk. He looked up, his eyes revealing nothing. "Anya. What brings you here?"

"I wanted to talk with you." She gestured toward the straight chair across from him, imagining the student athletes who occupied it, one at a time. Were they intimidated by this man who had once been in their shoes…um, sneakers?

"Please. Go ahead." He swept a hand toward the chair.

"Thanks." She sat, crossing her ankles to the side. Demure, businesslike. The chair squeaked as if to disagree. *Smartass.*

"Do you remember me talking about Zest, the online retailer where I work?" What a great grown-up voice. She was proud of it. The chair be damned.

"You mentioned it."

"From time to time, I do modeling for them." *From time to time.* That was a good one. Annie Sterling might say something like that.

"I'm sure you're a great model."

She hadn't meant to pause for a compliment; she'd better quit self-congratulating. "Thanks." She looked down and then back at him. "You said you're familiar with the menswear Zest sells."

Crap. Now he looked skeptical. She forged ahead, anyway. "So when I heard my bosses need a male model for a new men's collection that Federico Shampas is doing…" This time the pause was deliberate. Federico Shampas was a renowned designer, one of Zest's top "gets." Huh. No reaction from Ryder.

Hold on, did she really expect him to recognize the name of a clothing designer? He had picked up a basketball sitting next to his desk and was spinning it on his finger. "…I thought of you."

"Why?"

He was still very good at spinning a basketball. She watched his long, strong fingers and swallowed a sudden lump in her throat. "What?"

"Why did you think of me? It's not as though I have a long and illustrious modeling career. Or even a short one. Or even any interest in doing something like that."

So not going as she had hoped. Anya frowned. "Why not?"

"You don't get to answer a question with a question." More spinning of the ball. "Why did you think of me when that came up?"

"Because it would be a great opportunity."

"For who?"

"For *you.*"

"I don't understand why."

Did she have to find a chalkboard and write it out? She exhaled in frustration. "You already know you're a good-looking guy, Ryder. If you want someone to feed your ego, it's not going to be me." *Not a part of the plan. Going off track here.*

He pondered that and her, catching the basketball midspin and then sending it off again. "That's nice of you to say, but *if* it's true, which I'm not saying it is, there are a ton of good-looking guys out there. Much better looking than me. So why is this such a great opportunity?"

Because it's part of my make-Ryder-fall-for-Anya-instead-of-Annie campaign, you idiot. Okay, so she couldn't say that. "A lot of guys would jump at this chance. Pays pretty well for not much time."

"A lot of guys probably would. How many of them would be in wheelchairs?"

She frowned. "What?"

"Isn't that what this is about? Zest needs a disabled person in an ad, for whatever reason, and I'm the first person you thought of. It's not that I don't appreciate it, but come on, Anya. Be straight with me, at least."

"I am being straight with you. I pitched you, showed my boss your photo. I mentioned the wheelchair, but only because it makes you stand out from all the models, gives you an edge. Zest wasn't looking for *disabled*. That had nothing to do with it."

Doubt flickered across his face and then it was gone, replaced by the cool, vaguely amused mask she'd seen earlier. "Oh."

"Yeah. Oh. Get over yourself." So much for the grown-up voice.

He put the basketball down to shuffle a few papers in front of him on the desk. "I have a pretty full schedule." His tone left a question mark at the end of the sentence.

"You can make time. It's not like someone is going to come into your office and offer you this every day."

He looked at her long and hard. "But it isn't just someone. It's you."

"Is that the problem? It's me? Because I can have my boss call you instead. You don't even have to see me, I mean, it's not like—"

Ryder lifted his hand, telling her to stop. She did.

"I like seeing you," he said.

She strongly suspected the elated feeling that flooded her body at his words, pooling in her crotch, should have been a warning. But if it was, she didn't take it. "I like seeing you, too," she said, her voice squeaking.

"That could be a problem."

"Only if we allow it to be."

His gaze pinned her to the chair. Inside the coach's office, the temperature rose by at least ten degrees.

Damn. This plan may have been the best idea she'd ever had.

CHAPTER TEN

The test shoot was quickly scheduled. Only three days after Anya had been in Ryder's office, she was in the studio of the same photographer who had done her most recent photos, the ones set on the crumbling rooftop. At least this time, she knew where *not* to look, to avoid seeing that tattoo. Now that she understood what it represented to her, she didn't ever want to see it again.

The photographer was as warm and fuzzy as ever. "Where is this guy?" he demanded.

"He'll be here any minute." Anya had emailed Ryder everything he needed to know, including detailed directions to the photographer's studio. The only thing she hadn't told him—the fact that she would also be in the photos. That she would explain when he arrived.

She'd been up late the last few nights, talking with him as Annie, but she was also still basking in the afterglow of hearing that he liked seeing Anya. Four words, but she was holding on to them as tightly as the last piece of caramel candy in the store.

The door opened and Ryder came through it, his arms giving powerful pushes to the wheels. "Sorry I'm a couple of minutes late. There was an accident on the freeway."

Anya rushed to say, "No problem. You can't do anything about traffic." The photographer rolled his eyes. The stylist, a nervous woman with all the curves of a number two pencil and eyes that blinked furiously, emerged from behind her rack of clothes.

It felt ridiculously good just to see Ryder. A shivery excitement went through Anya. "The clothes are laid out over here." Her heels tapped across the wooden floor as she walked to the dressing room the stylist had set up with the clothes Ryder was to wear. With a flourish, she drew back the fabric curtain. "Really cool stuff. I think you'll like it."

"Since when does the model have to like the clothes?" the photographer grumbled.

"He'll like them," said the stylist. *Blink.*

Ryder glanced at the photographer and at the stylist and then turned back to Anya, following her to the dressing room.

"Do you need any help?" Anya touched her hand to her hair, a smile still on her face, though she was pretty sure it seesawed at the edges.

"You're offering to dress me?"

"If you—Sure. I mean, I didn't know whether—" Then she spotted the amused twist of his mouth. "No," she finished, looking down at the floor. It needed polish. But then, so did she.

"It's okay. I can dress myself."

"Of course. I know." She hadn't been that sure.

"You can go now." The twist of his mouth turned into a full-on grin, though it appeared as though he was trying his best to suppress it. He moved into the dressing room.

Anya drew the curtain behind him and glanced back at the hair and makeup woman, who was standing, hand on her hip, tapping the back of a hairbrush lightly against the palm of her hand. "What, you're not going to follow him in?"

"Not funny, Sandy," Anya muttered.

"Come here," Sandy said. "What is it with you and static? Your hair's standing up all over the place."

"Don't put any spray on her," the photographer grumbled. "She's already in the clothes."

"You think I don't know how to handle this, Jimmy?" Sandy snapped.

"James," he corrected tersely.

"Like I said, *James*, I need to get that hair under control or she's going to have a halo in your pictures."

"Like *I* said, *Sandra*, she gets one drop of hair spray on that dress, you're the one buying a new one."

Anya sighed. She'd bet this kind of thing didn't happen at Fashion Week. She walked over to Sandy. "Sorry, I don't know what happened. Guess I just have flyaway hair."

That fast, the hairdresser whipped a white cloth over her shoulders and began muttering to herself, while darting evil looks at the photographer. "I don't tell him how to take his photos, but he tries to tell me how to do my job. Thinks he's God and all. *James*, my ass. Only his mother ever called him that."

"Maybe he's just having a tough day," Anya suggested.

"Tough day." Sandy snorted. "He's been in a bad mood since 1999."

The stylist darted around the edges of Anya's personal space, checking her clothes.

"Back off, Margo," Sandy said. "The clothes are fine."

"I'll decide whether the clothes are fine." Margo took a step back, though.

Anya closed her eyes and mouth as hair spray enveloped her. Sandy's sharp jerks on the nozzle seemed directed at more than Anya's uncooperative hair. When the molecules had settled at last, Anya opened her eyes and asked, under her breath, "You've known him that long?" The man mildly terrified her.

"Longer, if you can believe it. But we've been married since ninety-nine."

"Oh?" Anya looked at her, at the photographer, and back to Sandy again. "Married. I've been afraid to even ask his name."

Sandy laughed. "Don't be. He's all bark." She carefully removed the cloth around Anya's shoulders. "Okay. Your hair's good again. Just don't mess it up."

Anya nodded, her thoughts veering back to Ryder. She knew how outside his comfort zone this would be, but it had seemed like a good idea. She walked to the dressing room and rapped lightly on the wood framing it. "Doing okay in there?"

She didn't hear an answer. What if he had fallen? Or was having trouble with the clothes? Or *hated* them and didn't want to tell her? She'd better hope the room didn't have an escape door. Jim or *James* would have her head, carefully coiffed hair and all. Not to mention Mollie. For all his bark, this photographer wasn't cheap.

As she was deciding whether to do a quick welfare check behind the curtain, Margo appeared at her side to yank it open. "You ready?" she asked Ryder.

He sat in the middle of the dressing room, bare-chested and in his shorts, examining the shirt he was supposed to put on. Anya sucked in a breath.

Oh, that body.

The athletic, powerful arms that had once held her so close, she'd never wanted him to let go. The strong, sculpted muscles of his chest, the brush of dark hair that came to a "v" just above his boxers. What was below those boxers—she remembered. *Too well.*

And his face. His broad, strong chin, sensuous mouth, and deep brown eyes, now staring straight through her. "Don't you people knock first?"

Oh. *Hell.* She had, hadn't she? She'd meant to. Crap. Now he'd think—he already did. She could see it in his expression. "Sorry." Heat crept into her cheeks.

"I don't." Margo looked at Anya and shrugged her shoulders. "Why should I? We're on a schedule." *Blink. Blink.*

"You want to invite anyone else in?" Typical Ryder. Sitting in only his boxers, but he didn't look at all fazed.

"No." Anya stepped inside, drawing the curtain shut behind her and leaving Margo on the other side. "Of course not."

She heard a protest from the irritated stylist and grabbed only enough of the curtain to peek around it and plead with Margo. "Give us a minute. Please."

The stylist threw her hands in the air and walked away. Anya turned back to Ryder.

"So just you," he said. "Let me guess, you *are* thinking you're going to dress me."

"I wouldn't—no." She'd actually been thinking more along the lines of *un*dressing him. "Besides, there's a stylist. That's her job."

"Try that again, without the lying part."

"Okay, so she mostly just chooses the clothes."

"Not that part."

"I wouldn't interfere. I swear. Not unless, you know, you need help."

"I do not." He put one arm through the shirt and then the other, pulling it across his chest. He began buttoning it, never taking his eyes off her, as though defying her to stop him.

She watched silently, the physical ache building inside her at the sight of his body, the body she had once loved so thoroughly. She missed him. Every single part of him. "I—" Had nothing to say.

Ryder finished buttoning the shirt and shook out the pants, lifting one of the now slender legs that had once sturdily carried him up and down the basketball court, zigging and zagging, baffling opponents who tried their best to keep up with him. He put one foot through the pants leg and then the other, and used his hand against the seat to lift himself from the chair to pull them up. It didn't work the first time; he had to do it again.

"Sorry. I have to—go." Anya fled the dressing room, yanking the curtain closed. She leaned against the wall, her breathing shallow and her pulse thrumming in her ears. Her heart squeezed tight.

She had done that to him. Put him in that chair. And now she'd put him in this studio, with the grouchiest photographer on the face of the earth, so that she could be close to him again, make him want her. Maybe even forgive her.

She was selfish, so selfish. Unbelievably. If she didn't have to *be* her, she wouldn't even *like* her. She lifted her chin and sniffed, forcing the liquid back into her eyes. Tears would help nothing; they could only make it worse.

"Something wrong?" the photographer asked. He didn't sound pleased by the prospect.

Another big sniff and Anya lowered her chin. She blinked as hard as Margo. "Everything's great. He's getting dressed. Will be out in a minute." She nodded, punctuating the words.

"Fine. Over here." He motioned toward the white backdrop he would use to photograph Anya and Ryder. "I want to set up the lighting."

Anya did as instructed, watching her step on the white fabric. She was wearing the newest Shampas shoe offering—a rounded toe with a Mary Jane strap and a pink metallic stiletto heel—that was driving Mollie crazy with apprehension. Mollie wasn't at all sure this shoe would sell, but didn't think the company could afford to say that to Federico Shampas, who was as notorious for his quick-fire temper as he was for his creative insecurities. So far, knock on wood, his offbeat fashion sense hadn't missed.

Anya turned her foot this way and that, trying to decide what angle would be most flattering. She had to admit, she sort of liked the shoes. Highly impractical and not very comfortable, but they were different than what she'd seen before.

The dress was short, in pink brocade, with a wide circle skirt and a triangular cutout, edged in metallic fabric, from just below her breasts to her waist. Sandy had used a darker pink eye shadow and blush when doing Anya's makeup, with a thick black eyeliner and mascara. Anya loved the entire effect—the gothic, sexy, cotton candy innocence that defined the signature Shampas look. It made it easy to pretend she was someone else, someone other than Anya Ramsey.

But she didn't. She already had one too many personalities to manage.

The curtain to the dressing room opened and Ryder came through it, headed toward the white backdrop. His wheels briefly hung up on the fabric, but he powered through it with an extra-hard push of his arms and came to an abrupt stop next to her.

"You look great," she told him. He did. The Shampas shirt and pants could not have fit him better. He looked classically and expensively well put-together in the untucked ice blue button-down and cuffed grey pants. On his feet, shiny black pull-on sneakers. In the Shampas world, men were a counterbalance to the women, a rock to their roll.

"Thanks," he said. "You look great, too."

"You really think so?" She watched him closely. Nothing but candor in his expression.

"I do. Like the dress."

So he was a fan of gothic cotton candy sexy. *Noted.*

"What now?" he asked Anya under his breath as the photographer moved his lighting around.

"We look like we're having fun," she whispered.

"Not sure that will work. These pants have a zipper that runs sideways."

Anya bit back a laugh. She'd forgotten about that. Federico Shampas, for some reason, liked to run the zipper on men's pants from the left hip to the crotch, instead of up and down. "Not comfortable?"

"Not comfortable. Pretty sure that part of me isn't built sideways."

This time, she couldn't catch the laugh before it escaped, earning her a scowl from the photographer. "I would remember if you were."

"Good to know," he said. A pause. "That you would remember, I mean."

"I remember. Everything." Anya stared straight ahead, not daring to look at him. The flashbacks were coming fast and furious. Her and Ryder, in his car, in her dorm room, in *his* dorm room.

The temperature was quickly rising in this place and it had nothing to do with lighting for the shoot. She shoved the memories aside, doing her best to rise to a higher consciousness, wherever or whatever that might be. "I'm wearing shoes that don't bend very easily. Sometimes you have to suffer for fashion."

"You, maybe. I'd much rather be in sweats."

And he had the best looking butt ever in sweats. She shook her head. Not a helpful thought. She pasted on a smile, ready for the camera.

"Remind me again why I'm doing this."

"Donation to the Conner High School Athletic Fund, remember?" she said, barely moving her smiling lips. Ryder had foregone the modeling fee, stipulating instead that it be donated. The athletes needed new weight-training equipment.

"All right. Look at me," the photographer growled. He pointed at Ryder. "What's your name?"

"Ryder."

The finger hovered in the air. "What, your parents rent trucks?"

Ryder's eyes narrowed. "Ha. Ha. Original."

Stupid photographer. Now she *really* didn't like him. "For your information, the name means 'Knight,'" Anya blurted. *"Jim."*

Ryder turned to her. "I don't need you defending my name to this guy."

"I wasn't defending, I was—"

"Whaddya say we get going with this fucking shoot?" James interrupted, thunderclouds darkening his expression. "Is that all right with you?"

"Sure." Anya drew her shoulders back. "Yes."

"Fine," Ryder said, throwing Anya a frown.

"You," the photographer pointed at Anya. "Next to him."

She moved close to Ryder's chair, striking several poses as the camera clicked away.

"Could we *try* to look like we're having fun here?"

Anya turned toward Ryder and leaned down until her face was at the same level as his. "Told you," she whispered, half turning away so the camera could catch the full effect of her playful smile.

"Nice, truck guy. Looking good." Rapid clicks.

"Thanks. I think."

"Alice," James roared. "You're giving me the same damn expression every frame. Change it up."

"Anya," she said.

"What?"

"Never mind." She went for a mixture of flirtatious and pouty this time. At least, that's how she hoped it came across.

She was so conscious of Ryder, she could barely concentrate. His clean, woodsy scent was making her think of moonlight, trees, stars in the sky, woodland creatures, and…God help her, an isolated hot springs with just her and Ryder.

"Alice. Mind on the game."

She pushed the thought aside and kicked into model mode.

Ryder had adopted an amused half smile. Anya knew, from photos they'd taken together in college, that he was one of those photogenic people whose pictures would be great no matter what he did. At the time, she'd thought it was a very cool quality. Now, with the crusty photographer yelling at her to change things up, she wasn't as crazy about it being so easy for Ryder.

"Come on, Alice," he said under his breath. "Mind on the game."

"Shut the fuck up," she responded sweetly, draping her arms around his neck.

"What the hell, you afraid of him or something?" James glared at Anya, then at his wife, who shrugged her shoulders.

"You're not showing the front of the dress." Margo the stylist, her lashes blinking like hummingbirds, darted into the shot to pluck at the pink brocade and rearrange both the cutout and Anya's left boob.

Dammit, Anya wasn't afraid of anything. Not a photographer who couldn't get her name right. Not a stylist who had no boundaries. And most of all, not Ryder, who seemed to be enjoying this debacle.

She turned her body and dropped into Ryder's lap.

"Ooof," he said.

"Let's try this." She put one hand behind his neck, the other on his chest and scissored her legs straight out, one of the shoes dangling from her foot. The feel of his skin against her fingers sent her pulse racing, but most of all, it was the feeling of his crotch against her backside that caused her to nearly stop breathing altogether.

"Finally," James said as he clicked away. "We get something going. Shift, though, so you're not covering up the shirt."

Anya wriggled into position.

Ryder didn't say anything. He didn't have to. Anya felt something stiff, and growing, against her butt cheeks. The "Hallelujah" chorus rang in her ears as she realized that something had indeed gotten going. Something large. Familiar. And most welcome.

She pressed her fingers harder into his neck. "That has to be *really* uncomfortable about now," she said, never letting her smile waver, "what with that sideways zipper, and all."

"Think you're pretty funny, don't you?" His voice had become husky.

"I think you might be enjoying yourself, after all." Euphoria, hope, and a thousand other emotions flooded her body and, throwing aside all caution, she turned to Ryder, put his face between her hands, and kissed him. James moved to one side and closer, the camera continuously clicking.

Ryder's breathing grew ragged under her touch. Anya's own breathing felt suspended by the sensation of his lips on hers. Warm and oh-so-sexy.

Then she heard the photographer's voice, close to her ear. "We interrupting something?" he yelled.

She screeched and jumped, startled by the sound and the pain of its proximity. Next thing she knew, she had tumbled to the floor, legs splayed, while James glowered at her from above and Ryder looked away, fumbling with his shirt, probably to make sure it covered his sizeable erection.

The light, fairly thin fabric Federico Shampas used for his men's pants would make a thing like that somewhat hard to hide. Which, all things considered, Anya was okay with.

CHAPTER ELEVEN

The photographer backed away at the same time Sandy the hairdresser and Margo the stylist came rushing forward. "Are you okay?" Sandy asked Anya.

"Fine. Yes." Embarrassed enough to sink through the floor and smarting from where her left butt cheek had made contact with the tip of Ryder's footrest, but otherwise, fine.

She looked up at him. He was still looking away, as though he would like to be anywhere, any place, but here.

James began putting away his camera equipment, snapping locks on cases with a vengeance. With help from the other two women, Anya pulled herself to her knees and then to her feet. "Thanks," she murmured.

"Did you get what you needed, do you think?" she asked James, hoping the answer would be *yes*. She'd put Ryder through enough for one day. "Or do we need to do some more?" What had possessed her to kiss him?

"No more." James shook his head.

"Okay," she said, uncertain, looking back at Ryder. He had started to wheel away, back toward the dressing room. "Wait," she called to him. She wanted to apologize for the shoot, or laugh about it, or do anything but not talk about it.

He didn't wait.

Oh, right. The transparent pants. She'd be lucky if he ever talked to her again. "You'll have these to Mollie tomorrow?" she asked James.

He nodded. "Don't worry," he said. "They're fine." He motioned toward Ryder's retreating back. "The camera likes him."

"I know." That was a relief. She might still have a job tomorrow. "Um, okay, I'm going to go now."

"Yep."

Margo was instantly at her side, hands flapping at her sides. "Just put the dress back on the rack. I'll take care of wrapping it up." *Blink. Blink.*

Anya nodded and teetered in the Shampas shoes toward the second dressing room, a smaller one than Ryder's, with a mirror that took up one wall.

She undressed, carefully placing the dress on the hanger, and put on her own clothes—form-fitting jeans, a T-shirt, and flats. When she drew the curtain back, Margo darted in to grab the dress and shoes. The stylist put the shoes into a box and zipped the dress into a plastic bag with swift precision.

Anya put her bag over one shoulder and tried her best to stay out of the stylist's way.

Next, Margo buzzed over to Ryder's dressing room. "Done?" she asked through the curtain.

Anya didn't hear his answer. She wasn't sure Margo waited for it before she slipped into the room and emerged a minute later carrying the shirt, pants, shoes, and socks Ryder had worn. By now, Anya also stood outside Ryder's dressing room, but Margo yanked the curtain back into place before Anya could see anything, and began stowing the clothing and shoes on the rack and in boxes.

Anya waited, unwilling to barge in on him again. She opened her bag and began looking inside, not because she needed anything, but because she didn't want anyone to think she was waiting for Ryder.

Sandy and James bickered back and forth at the door to the studio. When Margo moved between them to carry her rack of clothes outside, Sandy called to Anya, "Going to lunch. Last one to leave, lock the door, okay?"

Anya nodded. She glanced at the curtain to Ryder's dressing room. Still closed. She could wait for him to come out or…not. She walked over to tap on the wood, this time making *sure* she knocked.

"Yes?"

"It's me. Anya."

"Come in."

She did, to find him sitting in the middle of the room, fully dressed, and staring at a table holding a vase of pink carnations and several hairbrushes. After a minute, when he still hadn't looked at her, she asked, "What did you think of your first photo shoot?"

He turned, meeting her gaze. "I think you work with an interesting group of people."

"Oh." Half a laugh. "Well, they're good at what they do."

"You're going to have a hell of a bruise. You hit the footrest, didn't you?"

"Yeah, that." She put her hands behind her back and looked down at her shoes. "Doesn't usually happen."

"It's probably the shot they'll use."

"You could be right." She raised her eyes, feeling suddenly shy. "But you did great. The photographer said the camera loves you."

He shook his head. "First and last time I do this. I'm not a model. And those pants. Hell, nobody I know wears clothes like that." He had on a crisp, striped shirt and jeans, with black sneakers. And looked so good in them, a wicked heat began pooling inside her.

"Me, neither." She walked over to the table, straightening one of the hairbrushes, pulling a carnation from the vase. She held it to her nose, giving it a sniff and ignoring the drops of water that fell to the floor. "Only male models and designers."

"So who's buying the stuff?"

"Guys who want to look like male models or designers."

He made a sound of derision, but then smiled sheepishly. "When I said I liked the menswear Zest sells, I wasn't talking about pants with sideways zippers."

She could lose herself in his brown eyes, in the smile that crinkled at the corners and made her think things could be okay between them again. She laughed softly. "I know. That's not you."

He watched her intently.

Her breath caught. Suddenly, she didn't know what to do, how to act, what the protocol was. *Stick with the plan*, she told herself. *Be alluring, irresistible.* She parted her mouth and brushed the carnation's petals across them while envisioning dragging those petals down the length of his body, tickling him, arousing him, in all the right places.

She tried to make her eyes dance, because whenever she read about a heroine doing that in a book, the guy always seemed to be captivated. She could only hope her eyes didn't just appear jumpy and out of control.

"I'm beginning to worry about you."

Forget the dancing eyes. Bad idea. "What? Why?"

"Every time I see you, you end up on the floor. If you keep going like that, you're going to break something."

The flower's stem snapped between her fingers. She lifted her chin. "I'm not that clumsy." She laid the flower back on the table and clutched her hands in front of her.

A skeptical look. "Remember who you're talking to."

As if she could forget.

"Fine." She sighed. "So now you know. My coordination hasn't improved any since you saw me last."

He tipped his head to one side. "I'm not much help in picking people up off the floor."

She didn't know whether to laugh or to acknowledge the truth of that. So she simply said, "I'm sorry."

"Don't be. It doesn't come up that often. Except, apparently, with you." He grinned, causing butterflies in Anya's stomach to do backflips.

From outside the dressing room, Margo's voice sailed through the air. "Goodbye," she called.

"Oh." Anya raised her voice to answer, "Goodbye."

The door slammed.

The plan. Remember the plan. If only she knew how to implement it. That was the part she wasn't sure she had down. All she could do was try.

She straightened and walked over to Ryder. "Everybody left. Guess we're the only ones here now." She let her fingertips linger on his arm, then rise to brush against his shoulder blades. Very slowly. She felt him react, felt a tension in his shoulders.

He turned, watching her as her fingers came around to the front, traveling along his arm. His brows drew together in a "v." "Anya—" He broke off.

"Ryder, we had something incredible together once." She kept her voice breathy, soft, wishing she still wore the pink brocade dress he'd liked. "Don't you ever wonder if we could have that again?" Eyes locked on his, she reached behind to pull a chair beneath her.

"Things are different now." He didn't sound so sure. His voice had taken on a huskiness that hadn't been there before. She understood. That kiss, under the lights in the studio. Its intensity had taken them both by surprise.

She watched the rise and fall of his chest, the pulse jumping at his throat, and put her hands on either side of his face. "They don't have to be," she whispered. The skin of her palms sizzled at the feel of his rough whiskers. She leaned closer in what felt like slow motion. "I've missed you, Ryder."

"Don't do this." The warning was half-hearted, at best.

She ignored it and as her lips met his, she felt a thrill surge through her at the familiar taste, the deeply intimate play of their mouths on each other. He reached forward to put his hands on the back of her head, pulling her closer still.

The kiss became more urgent, more sensual as their tongues sought and touched. Anya had nearly forgotten how he could make her feel, as though nothing else in the world mattered but the two of them. All rational thought faded away so that she could simply melt into him and feel, rather than think.

God, she'd missed him more than she could ever say. Missed the way they'd understood each other, supported each other. Played. And loved.

She ran her hand down his cheek, down his chest, until it found the bulge in his jeans. *Yes.*

He abruptly pulled away from her, breaking off the kiss. As she opened her eyes, startled, he grabbed the wheels of his chair and pushed himself back, out of her reach. Her hands hovered in the air, helpless, before she dropped them to her lap. "What's wrong?" she whispered.

"This isn't going to happen." He sounded angry.

"I don't understand." She *would not* cry, would not let him see how his anger sawed through her like a dull knife.

"This isn't then. We aren't the same people. Too much has happened."

She heard his ragged breath. He'd felt what she had, dammit. In that second, she knew she wasn't going to cry. She was too freaking furious. "How long are you going to punish me? I made a mistake, a horrible mistake. It's been ten years. That isn't long enough for you?"

"How long," he repeated, his eyes boring into her.

"That's what I asked." It was hard to breathe, hard to think. Her cheeks burned.

"Until you can look at me without seeing what happened that night. Until *I* don't have to see it in your eyes."

Her heart wrenched, lurched. She pressed a hand to her chest. "That's not true." Her voice was so faint, she wasn't even sure she could hear the words.

"I don't need your pity."

"I'm not giving it." Desperation began tearing through her. "But what am I supposed to do, forget all about the accident? Act like it never happened? Tell me how the hell I do that. "

"I can't. And you're right." His voice was low and steady and it rumbled straight through her. "Neither one of us can forget and we'll never be able to. So it's better we move on."

"I don't want to. I want *you*."

He opened his mouth as though about to say something, but closed it again without a word. His face tight and jaw clenched, he maneuvered his wheelchair past her to the door of the dressing room. Then he stopped, hands on the wheels, and turned to look back at her. "We can't make it so it never happened. It did."

I tried, she wanted to scream. *It was* supposed *to never have happened. If Claire didn't love blueberries so fucking much, you and I would be together right now!*

"It was my fault," she whispered, her heart breaking a little more with each syllable.

"Don't you get it? My fault, your fault, it doesn't matter." He shook his head. "That was then. This is now. We could never have what we once did. The memories of the way it used to be would always come between us. If we can't forget that, we can't move forward." He pushed out of the dressing room, toward the door to the studio. "And we're never going to forget it."

Anya followed. She wanted to run in front of him, block the door, and prevent him from going out of it, but forced herself to maintain at least the appearance of self-control.

"I have to get back to the school. I have practice."

"Don't leave. Ryder, please. Let's talk about this some more."

"Like I said, I have to get back. Thanks for the"—he stopped— "experience," he said at last. "Hope the photos turn out okay for you." He opened the door and pushed through it. It closed behind him, with as much finality as his words had held.

Anya watched the closed door for several minutes, her mouth open, her scrambled thoughts racing. Until at last she sank to the floor in a heap and folded in on herself, hugging her knees to her chest, her head down. Anguish washed over and through her.

If it didn't matter whose fault it was, how was she ever going to make it up to him?

* * *

Annie Sterling wasn't online that evening. And she wasn't answering her text messages, either, though Ryder had sent several. Instead, Anya Ramsey was drinking wine and listening to classic breakup songs. A lot of wine and a lot of songs, each more strident than the last.

She'd just put on Whitney Houston's "I'll Always Love You" when she heard pounding on her apartment door. The sound startled her so much, she nearly toppled from the couch. Shit. Maybe Ryder was right. All pretense that she'd ever possessed coordination had finally left her.

She wove her way over to the door and threw it open to find Caitlin standing in the hallway. Anya leaned against the doorjamb, glass of wine in hand. "Hi."

"Hi. You look like hell."

"Thanks. So much." Whitney's voice soared in the background.

"Well, I can tell what kind of mood you're in." Caitlin moved around her, taking off her jacket and picking up the empty wine bottle on Anya's coffee table. Her eyes went from the bottle to Anya and back again. "Want to tell me about it?"

"No."

"Fine. I'll wait." She pointed at the bottle. "Got any more?"

"In the kitchen." Anya wasn't positive, but she thought a "z" or two might have rolled into her pronunciation of the word. And moving away from the safety of being held up by the doorjamb seemed a daunting proposition.

She remained in place until Caitlin reappeared, glass in hand, to close the door to the apartment and lead Anya back to the sofa.

"Why are you here?" Anya asked.

"Because you didn't answer my texts or my calls. I figured maybe the photo shoot didn't go so well."

"I had a plan."

"I know."

"I only have three weeks to make him not want to see Annie and want me, instead."

"Not very long," Caitlin agreed. She turned the volume down on Whitney.

"So why doesn't he want me? I used to be the only one he wanted." She strongly suspected she might be blubbering. And she didn't care. *Blubber on, sister.*

"I take it the plan didn't work very well."

"I fell on my ass."

"Figuratively, or…?"

"Both."

"Didn't that happen at the high school game, too?"

Anya glared at the other woman, as much of a glare as she could manage, anyway. "You're supposed to be my friend. You're not acting like it."

Caitlin shrugged. "It is what it is."

Anya jabbed her finger in the air. "*He* said that! He did."

"Okay. We're not getting very far here. And you have to work in the morning."

"Yes." Anya looked up. She could have sworn the word, *Yezzzzzzzz*…was floating somewhere above her.

"I'm making coffee."

"I don't want coffee. I want more wine."

"Too bad."

Anya let her head sink back onto the pillow, hoping both her jumbled, messy thoughts and Caitlin would disappear when she opened her eyes again. Another bottle of wine would help…

Instead, she felt a hand behind her head, lifting her up. "Hey," she tried to protest, to no avail.

Caitlin moved Anya's back against the sofa and put a mug of hot coffee in her hand. "Drink it."

Anya obeyed, her mouth pursing at the bitterness of black coffee. Once she'd drunk half the cup, her thoughts began to re-sort themselves into some sort of order, even if they were bickering amongst themselves for Anya's attention. Maybe she could outlast them by falling asleep for a week or two. She closed her eyes.

"What happened?" Caitlin asked.

Anya's eyes flew open. "I don't know how to act, how to be myself around him. I used to. Now I don't."

"Why?"

She stared straight ahead, at the nail still in the wall where she'd hung a picture she decided she hated and took it down, but never replaced. "Because every time I look at him, I remember I'm the reason he's in that wheelchair. The reason he didn't have a college or NBA career. Or a normal life."

"Did he say that?"

"Pretty much."

Caitlin needed empathy training, Anya decided. She really sucked at it and it was a very important quality in a friend. Critical, if you got right down to it.

"Are you yourself when you're Annie?"

"Yes." She took another long sip of coffee and thought. "Well, except for being a teacher and living in New York. That stuff. But otherwise, yes. It's me. Only better."

"That should tell you something."

"I'm tired of being told things." For once, she wanted to be the one to do the telling.

"Here's what that tells you. If you're yourself when you're Annie, you can be yourself as Anya. You're putting up walls." For the first time, Caitlin sounded uncertain. "I think."

"Thank you, doctor." The sarcasm she strove for didn't make it all the way into the words.

"Meet him over the Presidents Day Break, like he asked. Show him who Annie really is."

"I *can't*." The idea sent panic shooting through her. Not after the way things had ended today. He would turn around and leave before she could get two words out. She'd never see him again. That would be the last straw for him, to know that she had deceived him like that.

Bo got up from his dog bed and came over to her, shoving his wet nose into her flailing hand. She gave him a grateful pat on the head and a scratch behind the ears. "Sorry, boy. I'm okay."

"What are you going to do, then?"

"I don't know." She shook her head. "Wait. Yes, I do." She sat up taller. "Plan B."

Caitlin took a sip of wine. "Plan B," she repeated.

"Always have a backup."

"Not a bad idea."

"It involves you."

"I have a feeling I'm not going to like Plan B."

Another bracing sip of coffee. "It's pretty simple. You go to New York. Meet Ryder. It's your photo he's been looking at, so he'll think you're Annie."

"That doesn't sound simple at all. It sounds like a problem. And I've never even met the guy."

"That's okay. Neither has Annie. But first, I'll make sure Annie in person isn't quite as great as Ryder thinks she is."

"This plan has holes in it. Great big ones you could drive a truck through."

"It'll be fine." The more she thought about it, the better it sounded. "I'm still going to be working to make things right up until then, and by the time he gets back, I'll look *way* better to him than Annie Sterling. Who will disappear from his life as fast as she came into it."

Caitlin stared at her, wide-eyed. "I think you've lost your mind."

"That's okay." Anya was beginning to feel *almost* cheerful about this new approach. "It wouldn't be the first time."

CHAPTER TWELVE

Ryder looked up to see someone standing in the door of his office. He had to give his eyes a moment to adjust, as he'd just spent the last hour with the lights off, analyzing footage of the team's next opponent, but when his eyes finally did, they told him it was Anya standing there.

His heart did that leap that frustrated the hell out of him. This would never work. Every time he saw the guilt in her eyes, he felt his own. Felt it as a deep, sharp stab of regret that reminded him why she deserved better than him.

He was still angered by the fact he'd kissed her at the photo shoot. Twice. She'd started it. Exactly what had she been trying to accomplish? A pity fuck so she could make herself feel better about what had happened years ago?

She was better than that. *He* was better than that. But he'd kissed her back. And then some. If he had to face the absolute truth, which he didn't want to do, he would have gladly taken her right then in that dressing room. Pity fuck or not. That is, if he could have figured out the logistics in a way that wouldn't reinforce just how much everything had changed. He'd gotten better at figuring that out over the years, but only with women who hadn't known him before, hadn't known him when he had two legs he could use.

Getting angry helped. Because if he didn't get, and stay, angry, all he could think about was how much he missed the Anya he'd known, the one he could tell anything to, share everything with. He'd never met anyone like her before and he never would again.

He could deal with that. He had for the last ten years.

Until she'd shown up again in his life.

It didn't help *at all* that she looked beautiful right now, standing there silhouetted in the light. She wore a red dress that hugged her curves just right and red lipstick. Her fair hair was shining and loose around her shoulders.

"Hi," she said. "Can I come in?"

Anyone else who had this woman at his door would be tripping all over himself to invite her in and wondering how he got so lucky. Ryder glanced at the watch on his wrist, without noting the time.

"I've got about two minutes," he lied. He had at least twenty. No, make that thirty.

She walked toward him and set the envelope she carried on his desk. "Normally, we'd email these, but I thought you might like to see the photos printed out."

"Thanks. I guess."

"Don't tell me you're not curious."

"Fine. I won't. But I'm not." What was he supposed to do, frame a photo and hang it on the wall? Like hell. The athletic program would get money for the weight-training equipment the kids needed. That's all that mattered.

She sat down in the chair opposite his desk, even though the two minutes he'd allowed her were clearly up. "There's one I like."

"Great." He turned his attention back to the film now on pause, to make a point.

She didn't get the point. "Take a look."

He turned back. "Like I said, I don't have much time."

She opened the envelope and pulled out a photo. "This one." She slid it over to him. He had to put his hand out to stop it from flying off the desk.

He looked down at the eight-by-ten glossy photo. It was of Anya kissing him while sitting in his lap. Even though she'd surprised him, his eyes were closed and he was obviously enjoying the kiss. The sensation of her soft lips on his had sent his head and his heart reeling.

And that had been only a preview of the second kiss. The one that had come later, when they went from butterflies and hearts to waves roiling and crashing against the rocks. Damn good thing no one had taken a photo of that. It had taken him a long minute to pull back, away from her. His dick, though, had stubbornly held out hope for more. Traitor.

He still wasn't sure why he'd ever agreed to do this photo shoot. The Boosters Club probably would have given them money for the new equipment.

Maybe some small part of his ego had been flattered to think he'd been sought out for a photo with a beautiful woman, but now he saw what they'd really been after—a photo of a guy in a wheelchair to show how open-minded they were. Hey, look. We're so great, we're even going to pretend this guy gets the girl. Nice. Real nice.

"I hope that's not the one they're using on the website."

Anya bit her bottom lip. He'd hurt her feelings, which made him feel even crappier than he already felt. Before he could think of what to say, she spoke up.

"No. They're using one of the shots of you alone, that he took at first."

"Oh." That surprised him. Anya had looked sensational in that pink dress. He searched her face. "Are you disappointed?"

"Not about that." She shook her head. "It was a business decision. Happens."

She was disappointed about something else. He didn't want to ask and knew he shouldn't; his better judgment told him not to. "So what are you disappointed by, then?" It occurred to him that his better judgment frequently went flying out the window when it came to Anya. Always had.

She lifted a shoulder. "I thought maybe we could be friends again."

He glanced down at the photo. It wasn't his *friend* kissing him. When he looked back up, he saw that she had followed his gaze and was also staring at the photo. "Guess I didn't go about reconnecting with you in the right way," she said quietly.

He took a deep breath. "I don't think there is any right way. We're different people than we were ten years ago."

"True." Her eyes met his and held him transfixed. He'd never seen another person with eyes like hers, and the night after the photo shoot, when he'd closed his own, trying to sleep, the mental image of them wouldn't leave him. It wasn't only the unique shade of blue, it was the way she looked at him, as though he was so much more than he actually was, and the way his insides dissolved when she focused in on him, only him.

Too fucking bad she was still keeping a distance the length of a court between them, even as she passed him the ball.

"Guess I've overstayed my two minutes. You'll be late for— whatever it is you'll be late for." She stood.

"Practice," he said automatically, while fighting back irrational disappointment that she was leaving. He hadn't wanted her to come into his office in the first place.

"Practice." She nodded. "Another big game coming up."

"Huge game. To be brutally honest, I'm not so sure we can beat 'em." Okay, now he was just stalling.

"But you won't let the team hear you say that."

"Never," he agreed. "What they'll hear me say is that we have to get better at rebounding."

"And man-to-man defense."

He shouldn't have been surprised. Anya had been a student of the game. He'd always appreciated that about her. "Yes," he said. "And man-to-man defense."

A quick smile and then uncertainty in her eyes. "So, Ryder." Once again, she bit her bottom lip. "Can we start over?"

He wanted to say yes; he wanted to yell *no* at the top of his lungs. He had his career, he had his team, he had his friends. The last thing he needed was the complication of a former lover who came with enough baggage—most of it because of him—to fill an airplane's cargo hold.

As he searched for the right words to say, she reached out to take the photo from his desk. Holding it high, she tore it in half, right down the middle and then set it back down. "We can forget that ever happened."

Yeah, right. Tell it to his dick. Good luck with that.

"Come on, Ryder. Friends. What've we got to lose?"

Everything I've worked so hard to leave behind.

She extended her hand to him. After a second's hesitation, he took it, feeling her soft skin, her warm fingers, against his. They shook.

"Good," she said. "See you at the game."

Oh hell, no. If he knew she was there…He shook his head. "I don't think that's a good idea."

"But you just said we could start over."

"Right. But, no. I'd rather you didn't come to the game." He couldn't look at her, knowing he'd see hurt in her eyes.

"Fine. I won't."

"Thanks."

He didn't raise his head until he heard her turn to leave. Then he watched her long legs swiftly glide through the hall and disappear around the corner. Once he was sure she wasn't coming back, he looked down at his desk and slowly pushed the two pieces of the photo back together. Another quick glance up and then he rifled through a desk drawer to find a tape dispenser.

He rolled off a piece, cut it on the metal teeth, and placed it over the tear. It just…didn't look right, torn apart like that. He slid open another desk drawer and placed the photo in it, under a stack of papers.

He'd throw it away. Burn it.

Later.

* * *

You sound stressed. Tough day? Annie/Anya texted.

Watched so much film my eyes are crossing.

That worried about the game?

Yeah. That worried. Tough opponent.

You'll pull it off, Coach.

It took a minute for his text to come through. *Thx for the confidence.*

You'll find the right words.

Need the right strategy.

You'll find that, too. I believe in you. She did. She always had. *And I believe in your team.* Now she felt like a character in a Disney movie. She considered that. There were definitely worse ways to feel.

So you're thinking I should go Gordon Bombay on them?

Anya grinned. Of course. *Mighty Ducks.* That's why she'd felt so Disney-ish. *I believe in you, win or lose.* She flashed back to watching both *Mighty Ducks* movies with Ryder in his off-campus apartment, flicking popcorn at him while he mouthed his favorite quotes. By his own admission, he'd seen each movie fourteen times. Before the accident, she had to have watched them another six times with him, at least.

They're bigger, they're stronger, they're faster.

A test. No problem. She could pass it. *They've got more facial hair!*

Didn't think it was possible for you to get any hotter.

Her grin stretched so wide, it hurt her cheek muscles. *Yeah, well, just remember. A team isn't a bunch of kids out to win.* She must have watched those movies more than six times to be pulling these quotes out of her brain so easily.

He answered immediately. *A team is something you belong to, something you feel, something you earn.*

You and your team will do great. Good luck. Better uncross your eyes first, though.

Done. Thx for the pep talk. Did you book your flight?

Anya's stomach turned over. She'd managed to convince Ryder that Annie should make a trip from New York to L.A., instead of him going to New York. She had two and a half weeks until he would expect to meet Annie.

She still hadn't figured out how she was going to handle that, how exactly she would make sure Caitlin would turn him off Annie for good. On the other hand, maybe she would just let Cait be Cait. She personally adored Caitlin's no-bullshit approach, most of the time, but the woman did offend at least half of their coworkers at Zest on a regular basis. She wouldn't be Ryder's type at all.

She hesitated only briefly before typing, *All set. Can't wait.*

You can catch a Wave Riders game while you're here.

Ryder played for a wheelchair basketball team and updated Annie on the score after each game. She'd teased him about the name but, as he'd pointed out, it was a coed team so needed to be acceptable to both genders. *Wave Riders* was the only one they'd all been able to agree on.

Wouldn't miss it. Have a favorite player.

It would be Caitlin watching him, though, pretending to be Annie. That might not be such a bad thing. Anya wasn't sure she could handle seeing crashing, tipping wheelchairs and remembering when she'd only had to worry that Ryder would wrench a knee or sprain an ankle, not that he could be rolled over and lying helpless on the floor, unable to get up.

She wasn't proud of that, but then there wasn't a whole lot she was proud of these days. Why couldn't the do-over have worked?

Life would be a whole lot simpler if Madame Claire didn't like blueberries so much.

* * *

The Conner High School Wildcats ended up losing the game by two points. Anya knew that because she watched the broadcast on a local TV station and suffered through the relentless back and forth, up one minute and down the next, action until the final buzzer, when she sprawled out on her sofa, worn out from all the leaping to her feet and screaming encouragement while Bo hid in the bedroom.

Her throat felt raw and her fingers ached from the number of times she'd clenched them. She raised her head for a closer look when the camera zoomed in on Ryder, composed and professional despite the narrow defeat, shaking hands with and congratulating the coach of the opposing team. Her heart melted and puddled on the hardwood floor, next to the pop she'd spilled while celebrating Conner taking the lead in the second period.

Anya, pop, and Conner High School basketball didn't go together.

Ryder would be thinking only of his team and how he would help them through this. She wished, so wished, that she could have been there, but he'd asked her not to come. And she hadn't. If she could do nothing else right, she could at least keep her word on that.

She wanted nothing more than to talk with him, but she wasn't exactly sure what the rules of starting over were. And Anya didn't have his phone number to send him a text. But one person did. *Annie* could talk to him.

Just heard. Sorry about the loss, but your guys played fantastic. They must have a hella good coach. :)

A minute later, he responded. *Game just ended. How did you know?*

Oh. Right. This high school game wouldn't have been televised in New York. She thought fast. *Saw it on the web. TV station posted the score and said it was a close game.*

That was fast. I'm not even back to the locker room yet.

She put the phone down, worried she might say something else that could raise red flags. Then she picked it up again, typing out a quick message. *Be with your team. Talk w/u later.*

This wasn't good. Anya and Annie were beginning to trip over each other.

CHAPTER THIRTEEN

"But I hate coffee."

"You can't hate coffee. Annie Sterling drinks it all the time."

"It's disgusting."

"Get over it, Caitlin. It's not like you have to drink a ton of it. Just put it in front of you and pretend you're drinking it."

"Why are we meeting at Coffee Bean and Tea Leaf? Isn't the airport more logical?"

"Since I *live* here, I'm not coming in on a flight. And that's pretty hard to fake when someone wants to meet you at the airport."

"Right. Sorry."

"I told him I'm getting in late, will go straight to the hotel, and meet him for coffee first thing in the morning."

Caitlin pursed her lips. "So here's something. We have different voices. What makes you think he's not going to pick up on that?"

"Well…" Anya drummed her fingers on her desk. She hadn't wanted to explain this one. "I do your voice. On the phone, all the time."

"Are you kidding me? I don't believe it."

She demonstrated. "It's sort of a weird talent, mimicking voices. But I'm pretty good at it."

"You could have shared that talent before now, you know. Would have been great at the Zest Christmas party."

"Next year."

"Is that really what I sound like?"

Anya nodded. "It's a great voice."

"Sorta. Maybe." Caitlin sighed. "So what else do I have to know? And by the way, I hope I've mentioned that you're going to owe me."

"You've mentioned it. Believe me, I'm grateful. And you don't have to keep it up that long. Be a different woman than what he wants and everything will be fine."

"He wouldn't be going to all of this trouble to meet me, I mean *you*, if I was someone different than what he wants."

"I know." Anya chewed on her fingernail, a habit she'd thought she'd broken forever years ago. She hadn't been able to sleep for the last two nights, worrying about how this meeting was going to work.

"This is what to do. Act way too impressed with L.A. Tell him you swear you saw a couple of celebrities at the airport, or driving by you, or something. Pick names of actors you like, anybody, it doesn't matter. He'll hate that."

"Me, too."

"Just do it, anyway. And ask him if he'll take you on one of the bus tours of stars' homes. You know, because you want to see where they really live."

"I suppose I should also tell him I think the pollution is good for my skin."

"If you want," Anya mused. "You could say you're thinking of giving up teaching to try and make it as an actor. You just had a feeling it was your true calling when you landed and saw the palm trees and sunshine."

"Wow. I'm a winner."

"You could ask him if he knows anyone in the business he could introduce you to."

"Does he?"

"His father does, but Ryder stays away from all of that."

"So she's a teacher, which I'm not. She has a dog, which I don't. She loves basketball, which could be a problem because I don't. I don't even know much about how to play it. She loves coffee, which I hate. Anything else I should know?"

"Let me think." Anya tapped her finger against her chin. "Oh. You've seen the *Mighty Ducks* movies about a zillion times."

"Mighty what?"

"Ducks." Anya's eyes widened. "Disney. Kids on a hockey team. Coach with a huge chip on his shoulder. You've seen them, right?"

Caitlin screwed up her face, thinking. "No. Don't think so."

"You have to know them. You're meeting Ryder tomorrow morning. He won't believe you're Annie."

"So I'll fake it. Like I'm faking everything else."

"Not that." She drew in a deep breath. "You're coming to my place tonight. We'll get the movies on Netflix and watch them."

"But I don't want to watch Disney movies tonight—"

"You're meeting him tomorrow morning. You *have* to know this."

"People don't meet and start talking about movies. It's not gonna come up."

"It will. And you don't want to look like an idiot." Caitlin's hot button, she knew. Anya felt a little bad about pushing it, but only a little. This was important.

"I can't even believe you're putting me in this position."

"Thanks, by the way."

"You're going to owe me *so* big," Caitlin said, exasperated. "We're talking Grand Canyon big. I'm practically going to own you."

"I know."

* * *

Anya thought she had prepared herself for what would happen when she saw Ryder meet Caitlin for the first time. It turned out she hadn't.

When she saw the broad smile he gave the woman he thought was Annie, she nearly bolted from the spot where she had safely hidden behind sunglasses and dark clothing to shout, "Stop! She's a fake!"

Which made for an interesting conundrum, as the whole *idea* of Annie was a fake. Perpetuated by Anya.

So she stayed in her spot next to the window, in the coffee shop's outside courtyard. Watching the couple inside, she lifted a cup of coffee to her lips with a hand rendered unsteady by accelerated pulse and fight-or-flight signals coming from her brain. She had to wait for the plan to work, she told herself. It would work; it had to. This was just the beginning of it. Ryder needed to be completely sucked in by Caitlin/Annie before being turned off by them both.

And in a way, she should be glad he was so happy to meet Annie. Annie was, after all, Anya. In stealth mode.

She braved another look at them. She couldn't see much of Caitlin's face, but *could* see her friend curling a piece of her hair around one finger, a sure sign she was flirting. Jealousy stabbed at Anya. Death by a thousand sharp pinpricks.

She took a drink of her latte, stealing another look at Ryder over the edge of her cup. He was laughing now, his handsome features relaxed and at ease. She hadn't seen him like that since…since *before*.

A yearning began deep in the pit of her stomach and spread through her body until it lodged in the back of her throat, making it hard to swallow over the lump that formed there. Caitlin was laughing now, too. Anya watched as her hand reached across the table to touch Ryder's arm. That was *not* a part of the plan. Her assignment was to make Ryder like Annie less, not more.

Anya leaned forward, on heightened alert. She heard a bark from somewhere around her ankles, but ignored it. Then an unmistakable sniffing, with more barking.

"Coco!" said a woman's voice. "Leave the lady alone." The words were more of a coo than a command and clearly meant to attract Anya's attention. She didn't bite. She didn't have time right now to admire a dog.

Ryder put his hand out, touching Caitlin's arm. *What the—?* This was not supposed to be happening.

"I'm so sorry," said the woman's voice, a little louder this time. "My dog apparently likes you."

The woman didn't sound sorry at all. Anya glanced down to see a white furball with a pink bow on her head enthusiastically sniffing her leg. "It's okay. She probably smells my dog."

"Come on, Coco." The woman pulled on the leash. Coco, fascinated by whatever scent Bo had left on Anya's pant leg, paid no attention.

Anya lifted one shoulder and gave the woman a sympathetic smile before turning back to zero in on Ryder and Caitlin, aiming her gaze between the letters of the logo. Caitlin raised her cup of coffee, but didn't drink from it, instead drawing her shoulders back to puff her boobs out in her see-through shirt and give Ryder her lazy, you're-so-hot-I'm-about-to-undo-your-pants smile.

Anya knew that smile. She'd seen Caitlin successfully wield it many times. And she'd told her not to wear that shirt, which seemed a little much for a first meeting. What the hell was she trying to do? And how could Ryder fall for it? Anya had her nose smashed up against the glass before she realized it. She had to do something. Call Caitlin. And call her *off*.

Eyes still on the couple, she thrust her arm to one side, reaching for her purse, and in the process, knocked the paper cup containing her now-lukewarm latte off the table and onto the dog below.

Anya turned. Coco the dog barked as the liquid coated her white fur and glared up at Anya, milky coffee dripping off her nose.

"Oh no!" said the woman at the other end of the leash. "Oh Coco!" She grabbed napkins off the table and began furiously wiping down her dog with them.

"It's not hot. At all," Anya said. "I'm so sorry, though."

"This is awful." The woman deposited a soaked napkin on the table and picked up another one to do the same thing. "She was just groomed this morning."

"At least there was milk in it?" Anya ventured. "Or she'd be...darker."

"You think this is funny?"

Anya had opened her mouth to explain that she didn't, when she spotted the dog begin to move her nose and stomach to one side. "Watch out," she alerted, a second before the dog gave a vigorous shake to rid herself of the unwanted liquid.

It might have been somewhat funny before, as no harm was done to the dog, but it wasn't funny now. Coffee spattered in every direction, leaving cream-colored dots on the white silk top of the dog's owner. On Anya, the coffee that landed on her dark pants and top would only show temporarily, but she knew it would turn on her before long if she didn't sponge it off.

"I cannot believe this," said the dog's owner, staring down at her top. Anya had the uncharitable thought that maybe people shouldn't wear silk while walking their dogs, but she didn't voice it. "I'm sorry," she said again. She held out another napkin. "Maybe you should go inside to clean up," she suggested.

"Thanks for the tip." The women's tight expression said otherwise. Instead of taking the napkin, the woman thrust her dog's leash into Anya's hand. "I'll be back."

"Wait! I can't—" Too late. The woman was already barreling toward the door. Anya looked down at the dog, who returned the look with an expression that said she didn't like this, either. "It's only for a few minutes," Anya said, hoping the woman was a quick cleanup. She looped the end of the leash around her wrist.

The dog continued to glare at her.

"Really? Can I just say that this happened because you wouldn't leave my leg alone? You don't get to judge now. Maybe next time you'll keep your nose where it belongs."

The dog barked, a sharp, irritated sound Anya translated to being the dog equivalent of *Fuck you.* "Nice language, Coco."

A man sitting down at the next table glanced over, a quizzical look on his face.

Anya dipped her chin in a nod, as though nothing at all were wrong, and turned back to the window. Movement inside the coffee shop caught her attention. Ryder and Caitlin were coming toward the door. Caitlin opened it, letting him pass through before her. They both had big smiles on their faces, which put an instant frown on Anya's. She didn't like this whole thing. At all.

She ducked her head and lifted the book she'd brought, hoping they'd pass by without noticing her. Caitlin had no idea she was here. At her feet, the dog began sniffing again, alternating with a whimper. "Seriously?" Anya hissed from behind the book.

And then the dog bolted, so suddenly that Anya's wrist, holding the leash, jerked her forward and out of the chair. Her book went flying toward the puzzled man at the next table. Coco directed frenzied barking at her owner, who had reappeared in the doorway of the coffee shop. Standing directly behind Ryder and Caitlin, who turned to stare at Anya.

"Oh, my poor baby," said the woman, reaching for her dog. "What did that woman do to you now?"

Anya rolled her eyes, slipped the leash from her hand and gave it back, rubbing her now sore wrist and standing awkwardly, not sure whether she could pull off this being a chance meeting. Looking at Ryder's face, which contained the expression one might turn on a stalker, she decided the answer was no.

She accepted her book back from the man, murmured thanks, and then lifted a shoulder in Ryder's direction. "At least I didn't fall down this time," she said.

CHAPTER FOURTEEN

"Anya," Ryder said. "What are you doing here?"

"Having coffee." It sounded normal enough.

He looked skeptical. She didn't blame him.

Caitlin, playing her part, asked, "Is this a friend of yours?" She smiled sweetly at Anya, who seriously wanted to kill her.

"Oh. Yes." He sat up straighter. "Annie, this is Anya. Anya, Annie."

Holy shit. He was actually introducing her to the fake online persona she had created. This could not get any weirder. "Hello, *Annie.*"

"So nice to meet you." Caitlin extended a hand, which Anya gravely shook, though she couldn't resist a small dig of her fingernail into her friend's palm. "Oh!" Caitlin yipped. She recovered to add, "Strong grip you have, Anya."

"On a lot of things," Anya answered.

Caitlin lifted a brow.

"Coco and I are leaving," announced the dog's owner with a sniff. "Just so you know, I'm going to the dry cleaner. And Coco is going back to the groomer."

"Sorry. Again." Anya's voice was faint. "I'll pay?" she offered to the woman's back.

The dog's owner lifted her hand in a clearly irritated *never mind.*

Ryder watched the woman leave, then turned back to Anya. "I probably shouldn't ask," he said, even as he shook his head.

"Probably not."

"But you're right. At least you didn't fall down this time."

"There is that."

"Holding a dog hostage is a whole new side of you."

"There might be a few things you don't know about me."

"There are a lot of things—"

"Well, hey," Caitlin interrupted brightly. "Ryder is taking me to see him play basketball and then to dinner, so we'd better get going."

Anya bit down on her bottom lip so hard, she was pretty sure it drew blood. "Really?" she managed. Caitlin would get to see Ryder play for the Wave Riders. As much as Anya didn't think she wanted to see that, at this moment, she couldn't think of anything she'd rather do with Ryder.

Well, one thing. But that wasn't on the table.

Ryder appeared uncharacteristically at a loss for what to say. He plucked at his denim pant leg and then looked away, toward the parking lot. Finally, his gaze met Anya's again. "We met online," he said. "This is the first time we've been together in person."

I know. "Oh. That's great." To Caitlin, she said, "You don't live here?"

"Um, no. I do not."

"Going to do some touristy things while you're here?" *Go with it, Cait. Say the things I told you to.*

"I don't know, I'm not really into that kind of thing," Caitlin replied with a breezy smile. "Think I'll let Ryder decide what we do."

Caitlin would regret this, Anya vowed. A hammer. A candlestick. Colonel Mustard in the kitchen with poison. Friendship only went so far and Cait had not only run through the boundaries, she was jumping up and down on them.

"See you, Anya," Ryder said. He looked uncertain, as though he wasn't sure he should go. His hand was on the wheel, but he wasn't moving it.

Anya took a step toward him.

Caitlin grabbed the handles and began pushing him to the parking lot. "Bye, Alice," she said cheerfully.

"Anya!"

"Oh, sorry. *Anya.*" A wave goodbye, then Caitlin turned back to mouth, "He's so *hot.*"

Yes, definitely poison. It would make her suffer longer. Anya watched them leave, knowing she had created this disaster for herself and wishing she could do something, *anything*, to fix it.

She wondered if anyone, in the history of time, had ever made a bigger mess of a do-over.

* * *

Anya tried Caitlin's cell over and over before her friend finally answered, more than an hour later "Hey," Caitlin said, as though nothing in the world was wrong. When everything was. The background was noisy, with people laughing and what sounded like a PA system.

"Where are you?"

"Hold on a minute."

Easier said than done. Anya tapped the toe of her shoe against the floor, waiting. Bo padded over for moral support. She scratched behind his ears, her shoe tapping faster.

After a couple of minutes, Caitlin came back on the line, her new location quieter. "We're at the basketball game," Caitlin said. "Which is where I told you we were going."

"Why? Why are you there?"

"He invited me."

The condescension in her voice set Anya's teeth on edge, but not nearly as much as Caitlin's next comment.

"You should have told me how hot he is. I might have negotiated for something different. At least a few dates before I had to tell him." A giggle.

Anya's stomach tightened. "You have got to be kidding me."

"Relax. Of course I am."

Anya didn't realize she'd been holding her breath until she let it out.

"But I am at the game," Caitlin continued. "It's great. Why did I never know about this? There are cute guys all over the place. And the muscles. These guys are ripped. The game is good, too."

"You don't even know basketball." Anya shut her eyes tight.

"Don't have to. It's fun to watch. And not just for the muscles."

"The plan. You didn't follow the *plan*." Anya's voice rose. "You were not supposed to hit on him. You were supposed to make sure Annie wasn't the person he thought she was."

"How do you know he's ready for that? *You're* not even ready for that."

"That's not true."

"It so is. You relive that accident every day."

"I—you're wrong. I moved on. And you're going back on what we agreed on."

"You haven't even been able to go back to where it happened. You told me that. It's too painful. How is that moving on?"

"I don't have to go back there to move on." She sounded like a petulant four-year-old. Not what she was going for.

Caitlin's voice softened. "Just think about what I said, okay? I've gotta go. It's the half-inning. Or something like that."

"Halftime."

"That. He'll be looking for me. I mean, Annie."

"Caitlin."

"Bye. Talk to you later." She was gone.

Any flopped onto her sofa and punched the pillow. Once. Then twice. Then she rose up on her knees and pounded the pillow before she finally lay back down, exhausted, her arms aching.

Caitlin was now a former friend. She'd never trust the woman again. Anya would personally bust her in front of Ryder if that was what she had to do to get Caitlin away from him.

And she did *not* relive the accident every day.

Every other day, at the most.

* * *

Anya drove with a single-minded purpose, being mindful of the stoplights, the other cars, and any potential road hazards, while focusing her thoughts on her destination. No other thoughts or God help her, feelings, were allowed to intrude and derail her.

She'd spent the last several hours thinking about what Caitlin had said. She'd show her. Anya would go straight to that horrible traffic intersection and confront it, once and for all. What would Caitlin say then? Yeah. She'd say she'd been wrong.

Anya hadn't been back to that road since the accident had happened all those years ago. It was close to the college she and Ryder had attended and not exactly on the way to anywhere she went now. In fact, it would take her a couple of hours to get there. Besides, she knew side roads, even out there.

That intersection was like a wound that never quite healed, but if she could ignore it, treat it with aversion therapy, it remained a dull ache in the background. Or it had, anyway, until a crazy orange-haired woman with a blueberry fetish had opened it back up again. And then her alleged friend, who thought Ryder was *hot*, had brought it up again. Rubbed it in her face. Accused Anya of not being able to go back there. To a *road*.

As she neared her destination, her stomach began to churn and her chest tighten. Her cell phone rang. She glanced at the name on her dashboard. Caitlin.

She attempted to clear her dry throat and answered with a raspy, "What the hell do you want now."

"Calm down," her friend said, her tone unconcerned, despite their earlier conversation. "We finished dinner, so I'm calling you from the bathroom at the restaurant. I know you have a plan, but it's not like I can immediately make him not like me, right? That's not very believable, when we've been so close and all."

"*You* haven't been close with him. *I* have." Anya shoved her hair out of her eyes.

"That's what I meant."

"You were all over him at coffee." One of her hands, the one not on the wheel, clenched so tight, it made her fingers ache.

Caitlin made a clicking noise with her tongue. "Don't forget I was only playing the part you asked me to."

"I haven't forgotten anything. But what I saw wasn't what we talked about."

"Which begs the question, why were you there, anyway? We didn't talk about that."

Anya slowed the car for a red light and took a few seconds to answer. "To make sure everything went as planned."

"If I didn't know you better, I'd think you were jealous. Oh, wait. I *do* know you that well. And you *are* jealous."

"Caitlin…" It was growled as a warning; one she had no idea how to follow up on.

"Anya. I told you to relax. I'll carry out your dumb plan."

"That makes me feel better." Sarcasm oozed from her words.

Another un-Caitlin-like giggle filled the car. "You know, the funny thing is, I'm not hating this as much as I thought I would."

Anya blinked hard, then harder. "I know. You told me."

"Why did you ever let this guy go? Seriously, you dated guys like Zeke, instead? There's no comparison."

The hair at the back of Anya's neck lifted. "Cait—"

"Talk with you later. Don't worry, your plan's safe with me. It just needs some reworking, that's all." A click and the line disconnected.

Safe was not the word Anya would use.

She could not go through with the trip to the intersection. She glanced over one shoulder and made a rapid shift to the right lane, earning herself an irritated honk from the car she'd nearly cut off.

She flipped on her turn signal and peeled off at the next light, just three blocks from where everything had happened that ill-fated night ten years ago. Once she'd turned onto the side street, her shoulders loosened and she felt like she could breathe again. Until she thought of Caitlin and Ryder together, with Caitlin using the bring-him-in-easy plan she bragged about at every turn, and then everything clenched tight again.

She wove her way through the side streets until she came to a main road again. Spotting a Starbucks, she drove into the parking lot and pulled into a space, where she shut the car off and leaned back against the headrest, eyes closed.

Ryder couldn't fall for Caitlin; he just couldn't. But why shouldn't he? A lot of guys did. Caitlin was gorgeous and had literally charmed the pants off many a good-looking man, despite her lack of a filter. Most of the time, they weren't listening very hard to what she had to say. At least at first.

And Cait loved a game. That's exactly what being Annie represented to her. She'd take it all the way until it wasn't fun any more and then she'd drop Ryder so fast, his head and wheels would spin. Even if he didn't fall for Anya, he *couldn't* fall for Caitlin.

She opened her eyes and rummaged through her bag, looking for the business card Madame Claire had given her. She found it and dialed the Seattle cell number on the card, hoping against hope the woman was still in the vicinity.

After what seemed like an hour, but was only a few rings, Madame Claire picked up. "Yes-s-s?" she answered. "Who is it?"

"Anya Ramsey."

"Oh."

"Yes. Oh."

Silence on the other end.

Anya plunged ahead. "You have to fix this. You screwed it up, now you have to make it right."

"This I cannot do." The woman's voice was calm, certain.

Anya would not, could not allow her to dismiss this. "I don't believe you." The last word came out in a gasp. It hurt to breathe.

"This I am sorry for, that you do not believe me. But it would be far too dangerous for me to attempt such a thing."

"As if it wasn't dangerous in the first place?" Anya pressed a hand to her forehead. Her palms were beginning to sweat. "It didn't bother you to attempt it then. You were all over messing with someone's life. *Two* someones."

"That is the thing. If you will."

"I *won't*."

Madame Claire continued on as if Anya hadn't spoken. "There can be other consequences. That one is hopeless to predict. As of now, this face of yours, it is fine. You are fine."

"No. No, I'm not."

"And the man you were with, he is the same as he was. No worse."

"That's what is wrong. That's what you have to fix. You promised me you would."

"Ah, but it was your do-over, was it not? Your wish. That came from the part of your heart most true. This tells me the fixing of your face was more important."

Anya covered her eyes, pressing her fingers into the lids to hold back the tears. Didn't work. They spilled out, anyway, leaking onto her cell. "*No*. If the accident had to happen, I would rather he not be paralyzed and my face still be scarred."

Madame Claire didn't say anything. Anya could hear her breathing. "Please," Anya said. "I would never want that. I'm not that person. He's my love, my soul. He doesn't deserve what I did to him."

"But if I were to attempt this again, it could be worse. He could be killed. You could be killed. And all would be lost, never to return."

Anya felt the energy leave her body, leaving her sinking in on herself in the leather seat. The busy activity in the Starbucks parking lot lessened, as though the world were now moving in slow motion.

She tried once more, but this time, her heart wasn't in it. "Even if there were no blueberries to distract you." She would never eat the fruit again.

"No blueberries. Yes. Even if."

The only thing worse than being responsible for Ryder's paralysis would be his death. At even the thought, Anya felt a part of herself crumble up and die. She shivered.

"Perhaps…" Madame Claire began, making the word sound like pear-hops-s-s. "You would look inside yourself. The leaving out of a small part of the spell, that meant you would remember what had happened when you should not have. It did not make the do-over happen as it did."

Anya did not like where this was going. She would never have wished for her face to be free of scars over Ryder being able to walk. *Never.* Would…she? She quickly changed the subject. "So if it's all down to my wish, then no one would be killed, *could* be killed if you did it again, right? That's what you're saying, isn't it?"

A clucking of the tongue. "The first time, yes. The second? No, no, no. Most dangerous. No one could know how all might unravel, not even my mother, who knows it all, she will tell you, and still she will not quit with calling me in the middle of the night." Now a huge sigh. "What is done is done. This I tell you and this you must believe."

"I see," Anya whispered. She didn't. Not any of it. But she knew a lost cause when it smacked her in the head. There was no way this psychic was budging. And even more importantly, no way Anya would take a chance with Ryder's life.

"All will be as it must." Madame Claire's voice sounded gentler than it had a minute ago. "That is how the universe works. We must learn to live within what we have been given."

Interesting philosophy from someone who had performed a do-over of what had been given. There was, apparently, only one thing left to say.

"Goodbye."

Anya disconnected the call. And buried her head in her hands.

CHAPTER FIFTEEN

The next night, Anya sat cross-legged on her sofa, watching *13 going on 30*. Bo's head lay in her lap, his warmth comforting and calming. The dog periodically looked up at her, his eyes searching her face for a sign that she was okay. She stroked his head and his soft ears, wishing she could give him that sign.

Beside her on the table lay a bowl of untouched popcorn, a stack of napkins, an open bottle of reasonably good wine, and a glass. As she didn't have an appetite for eating anything, she didn't need the napkins, and she wasn't sure she could trust herself with the wine. It would either give her the false courage to do something she would regret later, or it would muddle her mind and put her to sleep.

The mind-muddling was an attractive option, but she needed a clear head. Once the movie, one of her all-time favorites, was over, Anya had scheduled a come-to-Jesus meeting with herself. And it wasn't going to be pretty. Which was why she was delaying as long as possible.

In the movie, the music from "Love is a Battlefield" began playing, and Jennifer Garner leapt on the bed to lip-synch the classic anthem with her teenage friends. Anya had been waiting for this part.

"Excuse me," Anya said to Bo. Gently, she lifted his head and laid it back down on the cushions. Then she stood, further down on the sofa, and joined the actresses on the screen to wave an imaginary microphone in front of her face and shout along with the music, "We are young, heartache to heartache."

Bo, familiar with this one, watched patiently, his head bobbing up and down with the movement of the cushions.

"We are strong," she sang, "no one can tell us we're wrong."

At the end of the scene, Anya sank back down on the sofa. And thought, as the movie continued to play. Could she have been as caught up in herself as Jennifer Garner's character? Could she have wanted only the best for *Anya*, even as she told herself erasing the accident would be all about Ryder?

Look at what she'd done with a career when there wasn't an issue with scarring on her face. Had she developed her art further, done more with her passion for animals, tried to make *anything* around her better?

No. She'd gone into a line of work that was all about how she looked. She angled for photo shoots she hoped would enhance her modeling career and had even maneuvered Ryder into doing one.

Anya turned the movie off. Bo raised his head, questioning. She headed for the bathroom, padding across the hardwood floor in her bare feet. On the way there, she picked up a black Sharpie from the table.

Standing before the mirror, she raised the Sharpie to her cheek, squeezed her eyes shut to grab the mental picture, and then opened them again to begin drawing. On her left cheek, right below the bone. A jagged scar with uneven edges, four inches long, nearly an inch wide.

The lines from the black marker stood out in sharp contrast to her skin. She hesitated, then filled in the lines, making the wound she'd drawn much worse, much more stark than the real one she'd carried on her face before the do-over. It seemed fitting. She had to evaluate the scar for everything it carried with it, which she suspected was a lot more than could be seen on the surface.

If she'd never been given the opportunity for a do-over, she would have this scar. She would be working as…as…she couldn't quite put her finger on it…Something with an actress. *There*. She had it. She'd been an assistant to an actress. A polite (raised in the South), but self-centered actress who sought the spotlight whenever and wherever possible, and lamented a perceived demise of her career… Every. Single. Day.

It had been mentally exhausting and not anywhere near rewarding, but Anya had stayed in the job. Hovered in the background as though she deserved nothing more, should want nothing more.

Punishment. That's what it had been. She'd punished herself daily for the accident and what had happened to Ryder. She'd worn that scar like some sort of brand that would mark her unworthy of happiness.

She'd made sure any relationships she had didn't last, telling herself she was only being pitied. But was she? She couldn't be so sure. It had been more important not to let anyone close enough so that she could tell. The last time she'd let someone that close, she'd paralyzed him. Forever.

It wasn't pretty, this looking inside stuff. Even worse, Anya wasn't the person she wanted to be before *or* after the do-over. That meant—that meant something was wrong. She'd been looking for forgiveness from Ryder, instead of looking deep inside to understand why, *really* why, she needed it.

Her cell phone buzzed. At first, she wasn't going to answer it, but then she wondered if it could be Caitlin calling about Ryder. She shut off the bathroom light and walked back into the living room.

Caller ID showed it was Zeke. She expelled a breath in frustration. Saturday night hookup. Talk about punishing herself. She pressed ignore, mulling over the new insights that helped her know how it was she'd been as bad at relationships in this new, done-over life as she had been previously.

Not worthy. She'd thought herself not worthy. It was one thing to understand that, another to do something about it.

"Where do I start? What do I do?" she implored the ceiling.

Bo tipped his head. The ceiling gave no answer.

Enough. Anya grabbed her car keys. She knew one thing she could do that would help. It was now or never.

* * *

This time, Anya came closer to the intersection, a measly two blocks, before she felt the tightening in her chest, clammy palms, and beads of sweat forming on her forehead. She told herself that had to signal some kind of progress.

One block now until she reached it. One block. What if she hadn't gone that way when she'd driven Ryder away from that party ten years ago? She now knew how many other routes were available, along the side streets, even if she hadn't realized it then.

Side streets. She didn't *have* to do this. She probably *couldn't* do this. Abruptly, she shifted to the right lane and breathed a sigh of relief that there wasn't another car when she did. One block. She signaled and turned, away from the intersection, choosing a side road instead.

The further away she traveled, the easier it felt to breathe. That's when the anger took hold. The anger at herself, at the traffic intersection ruling her life. She pulled over, in front of one Southwestern-style house, in a row of similar houses. A man walking his dog peered at her with curiosity. She looked away, focusing on a mailbox painted with flowers.

She could do this. She had to do this.

So she tried again. And again, each time making sure she was in the left lane and each time losing her nerve and switching to the right lane so she could turn off at the same side street. On her fourth try, a car was in the right lane, even with hers. At the instant she panicked and tried to move, the car was there. She couldn't change lanes without hitting it.

She came closer to the intersection. She honked at the car. Its driver responded with a flash of his middle finger against the window.

Oh God, she was going to do it, whether she wanted to or not.

The intersection was upon her now. The one that had caused two lives to change forever in the blink of a missing green arrow. She was here. She was about to die. She could hear her heartbeat drumming in her ears and feel the tension running through her body, even as her knees turned weak.

Around her, cars drove as though it were any other normal night, any other normal road. The light ahead of her turned yellow, then red. Anya slowed, having to press harder on the pedal with a leg that had turned shaky and unreliable.

Her eyes glued on the light, she focused on nothing else. Not the sound of an accelerating engine as cross-traffic went through the other way. Not the thumping sound of bass coming from a car nearby.

Just waiting until the light turned green and driving on her way, out of danger, out of her past.

It took her a few minutes to realize she'd actually done it. She'd stepped on the gas, slowly and carefully, when the light turned green and she'd driven through the intersection and several blocks past it, without incident. For the first time in ten years. And no one had died or been injured.

She circled back and did it again, to be sure. A giddy sense of relief began to wash over her, but quickly subsided when she realized she hadn't turned left in the middle of the intersection, as she had that night. She couldn't allow herself to feel she'd truly faced this fear until she'd done that.

She inhaled deeply through her nose, then exhaled through her mouth. Did it once again, then lifted her chin and turned the car back around for another pass. The streets were quiet around her, dark houses showing it had grown late enough that people had gone to sleep, safely tucked into their beds and unaware that outside, a woman was resolutely driving through an intersection that had once terrified her. Again and again.

She moved into the far left lane this time and turned when the green arrow made its appearance. Then she went back around and did it another time. The third time through, she waited until the arrow had gone and only the green light showed. With each pass through the intersection, there were fewer cars around her. That did nothing to ease her nerves as there hadn't been many cars on that night, either. Just one other, and she hadn't seen it.

At last, she felt she had had enough. She pulled her car onto a side street, pushed the gear into park and sat, head in her hands, the engine running, for several minutes. Above her, the harsh beam of a streetlight shone through her windshield.

It helped, coming back. Helped her see that it was just a street. A street where a very bad thing had happened, years ago. A mistake made by a teenager who was upset, not focused on where she was going and what she was doing.

People made mistakes. She'd forgiven herself for other mistakes, but not this one. Never this one.

She laid her head back and closed her eyes. The guilt, the pain. It felt so much worse since the do-over, since she no longer bore a scar. She raised her fingers to her cheek and touched her skin where she'd drawn on it with the black Sharpie pen. When she pulled them back again, she saw traces of black ink on the pads. Not surprising considering she'd broken out in a cold sweat on all of the early passes through the intersection.

It occurred to her that she'd never apologized to Ryder. At the realization, she bolted upright. Could that be right? *Never?*

She flashed back to when she'd tried to visit him in rehab. Before the do-over, he'd been so furious with her, he'd heaved that water bottle at the wall. After the do-over, he'd been detached, distant.

She'd never once told him she was sorry. Before *or* after the do-over.

From her bag, she heard her phone buzz. She pulled the phone out and couldn't believe the name she saw. Ryder. A thrill ran through her. This had to be a sign that what she'd been thinking was exactly right. She had to apologize. It was a sign.

She looked at the message he'd written to Annie. *All I can say about tonight is, amazing. Worth the wait. Wish you could have stayed the whole night, but I get the early morning thing. See you for lunch. At our place. XOXO*

Her throat constricted. Worth the wait. What the fuck had been worth the wait? Wish you could have stayed *the whole* night? They had a *place*, without her?

She glanced at the clock on her dashboard. One thirty a.m. One freaking thirty. A. M. He could have only meant one thing.

She might not have been serious before, but she was now. If Caitlin had slept with him, and it sure as hell sounded as though she had, Anya was going to kill her. With her bare hands.

How *could* she?

Hands trembling, she dialed Caitlin's number. No answer. This was not happening, *not* happening. Caitlin couldn't, wouldn't do this. Not to her best friend. Not to Ryder, who was innocent in all of this deception. He though Caitlin was Annie, the woman he'd become so close to online.

He had no idea Caitlin had taken advantage of him. She flashed back to Caitlin's casual, conspiratorial remarks about how hot she thought Ryder was.

Anya's throat was so dry, she couldn't swallow. She might not be able to swallow ever again. Not that it mattered. Once she was in prison for doing Caitlin in, she wouldn't want or need to swallow.

She jammed the car into drive. Caitlin, her former best friend, had been able to get away with a lot in life, but she wasn't going to get away with this. She would not play with Ryder's feelings and throw him away. Not if Anya had anything to do with it.

Anya planned on having everything to do with it.

CHAPTER SIXTEEN

Anya pulled up in front of Caitlin's apartment building with a screech of tires. She didn't care. First of all, it was nothing short of a miracle there was street parking in front of the building and second of all, there might as well be witnesses to Caitlin's demise.

She pictured a confused neighbor squinting into a TV camera. *"I'm pretty sure I heard a car around one thirty or two. Tires. You know that sound. I turned to Harry and said, 'Did you hear that? Someone is sure in a hurry.'"*

Someone was most definitely in a hurry. Anya got out of the car and slammed the door. Might as well let the neighbors hear that, too.

The street was silent and, to Anya's mind, filled with foreboding. To her right, a cat spotted her, froze in place, and then skittered to a hiding place. *Good decision.*

She strode to the front of the building and pressed the buzzer that would sound inside Caitlin's apartment. She waited, letting her gaze shift right and left down the quiet street. A lone car passed by.

No answer. Again she pressed it, letting her finger stay on longer, then lifting it and buzzing it again. Finally, she heard Caitlin's voice over the intercom. "Who is this?" She sounded snappish, irritated.

"It's me."

"Anya?"

"Yes. Let me in."

"Something wrong?"

You might say that. "Yes."

"Okay." The buzzer to the door sounded.

Anya slipped inside the door and then pressed the button to call the elevator. It came quickly, as most people in the building were asleep and not in need of the elevator. When the doors opened with a quiet ping, Anya stepped in, jamming the button for the fourth floor several times. The doors slid shut. Anya faced them, her hand clenching her bag so tightly, her fingers ached.

Ping. Second floor. *He might have been talking about her staying the whole night at the basketball team's after-party.*

Ping. Third floor. *He might have meant the food at whatever restaurant they went to was amazing.*

Ping. Fourth floor. The elevator doors opened. *Bullshit. He meant exactly what it sounded like. And now he's wondering why Annie hasn't answered.*

Her footfall through the hallway was heavy and determined. When she arrived in front of Caitlin's door, she pounded on it with her fist. *Nice Anya, kind Anya, is gone. Fucking furious Anya is here. Deal with it.*

The door swung open. "What is wrong with you?" Caitlin demanded. "Are you *trying* to wake up all of my neighbors?" She took Anya's arm and pulled her inside the apartment, closing the door behind them.

"I'll tell you what's wrong with me." Anya shook from head to toe.

Her friend folded her arms across her chest and shifted her weight to one side, waiting. She was dressed in her pajamas —a T-shirt and shorts. But she clearly hadn't been asleep yet. Her hair looked too good.

"Did you sleep with him?"

"Did I sleep with him," Caitlin repeated, drawing out the syllables. Her gaze, locked on Anya, was steady, unfazed.

Anya clenched her jaw, determined to keep her cool. "You heard me."

"Why would you think that?"

"*Annie* got a text from him. He called it an amazing night. Worth the wait."

"Oh." Caitlin's voice lifted and the hint of a smile curved around her lips. "Amazing?"

Anya's stomach hardened; her breath came faster. "He said he wished you had been able to stay the *whole* night."

Caitlin turned and sauntered to the bar at the end of her kitchen. She took two glasses from the overhead rack, pulled the cork from a bottle of already-open wine, and lifted the bottle to pour wine into each glass. The liquid gurgled. It was a generous pour.

Caitlin glanced back at Anya. "What's all over your face? Art project gone wrong?"

Anya's hand flew up to her cheek. She'd forgotten about the scar she'd drawn with a black Sharpie. "No. It's just—never mind." She walked to Caitlin's sink, pulled a paper towel from the roll on the counter, and ran warm water on it. Then she began scrubbing at cheek. "Tell me what happened tonight. Everything."

"I'm not sure you want to hear." Caitlin offered one of the glasses to Anya, who shook her head.

No. She did not want to hear that Caitlin had slept with Ryder. She'd been wrong, so wrong, to come up with this plan, to trust Caitlin, to keep Ryder in the dark. Tears welled in her eyes. She would not let them fall, just as she would not let the dagger plunge any further into her heart.

She'd made another huge mistake when it came to Ryder and this one was just as much her responsibility as the accident had been. This mistake, though, she might be able to fix.

"Do not hurt him, Caitlin. He's not like the other guys you date. He's different."

Caitlin lifted the glass to her lips and took a sip. "How so?"

"You know how so."

"Tell me. Go ahead. As far as I know, he's a guy. A hot guy, but a guy. Two arms, two legs, one mouth, one penis."

Anya's cheeks flushed hot. How dare Caitlin be so dismissive of Ryder. "He's one of the good guys and if you paid any attention at all while you were with him, you'd know that." Her words came faster, sailing through the air like virtual arrows. "Huge heart, thoughtful, kind, hardworking, smart, great teacher, great *mentor*, puts others first. Yeah, he's hotter than hell, but if that's all you see, you're missing a whole hell of a lot. Smart. Kind. Did I say that?"

Caitlin nodded and took another sip of her wine. "You did."

"Protective, caring. Fights his own battles. And wins. He's the guy you want by your side and he's the one who will always be there, holding your hand when things are bad and celebrating when things are good." She began hyperventilating and put a hand out, holding on to the counter for support, afraid she might pass out. *Not now.*

"So why are you telling me this and not him?"

Anya took a minute to get her breath back. "He's the one who—" Wait. What? Anya concentrated on slowing her breathing. "I don't know what you mean."

"Did you ever say that to him, tell him how you feel about him?"

"Of course I did."

"As Anya? Or as Annie?"

"As Annie—" She broke off. "Annie, Anya, what difference does it make?"

"Kind of a lot." Caitlin set her glass of wine down and walked over to Anya, putting her hands on Anya's upper arms. "You idiot." She said it with affection, confusing Anya even more.

"If you don't want to be Annie, don't do it. Just don't hurt him." She couldn't stand it if Ryder was hurt because of something stupid she'd done. And over the last few days, she'd done a lot of stupid things. Setting him up with Cunning Caitlin was only one of them.

Caitlin squeezed her arms. Hard. "Listen to me. Ryder knows who Annie is."

Anya blinked. "So do I. She's a teacher. She's—not you."

"I mean he knows you're Annie."

"No, he doesn't. You're lying."

"He didn't know at first. Actually, not for a while, I don't think. But then he started wondering about some of the things you said to him. And when you started talking on the phone, well, maybe you're not as good at changing your voice as you think."

Anya slowly shook her head. He'd known?

"You're the one who said he was smart. Twice, in fact."

"But—" She didn't know what to say.

"When we saw you at the coffee place..." Caitlin shook her head, and laughed. "You really shouldn't try that whole undercover thing. You're not very good at it. We saw you right away." She released Anya's arms and walked back over to the counter to retrieve her wine. "That's when he said he knew for sure and I guess he decided to test you tonight with that text. See if you would come out of hiding."

He'd decided to test her. A slow burn that began in the pit of Anya's stomach started to move its way upward. "Did you sleep with him?"

"Of course not." Caitlin looked offended. "What kind of a friend would that make me? You're the one who's in love with him."

Relief made a brief appearance in Anya's brain, but was quickly swept aside by fear. All she'd wanted to do was fix a mistake, but she discovered she'd fallen in love all over again with him, while posing as Annie. That didn't mean *he* was in love with *her*. How could he be? Look what she'd done to him.

Caused an accident that ruined his life, didn't talk to him for years, and then when she did, she pretended to be somebody else. Nobody in his right mind could love someone who'd done all that.

"He doesn't want anything to do with me."

"Yeah, you would think that." Caitlin yawned. "Turns out it's not true, though."

Anya fought hard to keep her hopes from lifting. "How do you know? Did you talk about it?"

Caitlin put a hand on her hip. "Well, we didn't talk about *me*. At first that sort of pissed me off, but then I went with the inevitable."

"Tell me what he said. Did he—? I mean, is he ang—? What did he say?"

"No way." Caitlin shook her head. "This is between you two. If you want to know what he thinks and he wants to know what you think, you're going to have to ask each other." She crossed the room, turning Anya toward the door and pushing her from behind. "Go home, get some sleep, and then go see him. You people need to talk. And I need to go to bed."

"I can't. I wouldn't know what to say." It would be easier just to let it alone, to have him make the first move. She tried plunging a pin into the hope within her that refused to be denied. It didn't work.

Caitlin opened the door. "As my mother always said, 'You made your bed. Now you're going to have to sit on it.'" She gave Anya a gentle shove through the door. "I don't know why she could never get that saying right, but I guess it still works." A tired smile. "You can do this. Pretend you're Annie, if you have to. She always seems to know what to do."

The door shut while Caitlin was still yawning. The last image Anya had was of her friend's tonsils.

* * *

Anya knew where Ryder lived. She wasn't nearly as bad at undercover work as Caitlin had made it seem.

She put the address into her GPS and, just past two thirty a.m., pulled her car to a stop in front of a smallish stucco house about a mile from Conner High School. All of the lights inside the house were out.

She let the engine run for a few minutes while she pondered what to do. She was wide-awake. Confused. Focused. Fearless. And scared to death.

A great start.

Anya was not a person who knocked on someone's door in the middle of the night. She should have done what Caitlin suggested, she thought, and gone back home for sleep before deciding what to do. Wouldn't have done much good, though. She couldn't fall asleep right now if her life depended on it.

She turned the key in the ignition and shut the car off. It was time. This was either going to go well or it was going to end up worse than ever. No in-between.

Everything around her was still as she walked up to the door of the house. It was as if the night was waiting, breath held, to see what would happen. Standing under the glow of the porch light, she knocked, quietly at first because the sound seemed to echo down the block. Then harder.

Nothing. This time, she pressed the doorbell and heard it chime inside, along with the sharp bark of a dog. There was a window to the right that ran the height of the door. She leaned over to peek through. Too dark to see. She rang the bell again. He might not be home.

A light flipped on and the door pulled open. A large German shepherd mix barked at her, demanding to know who she was and what business she had with his owner. This would be Stanley, she knew. Ryder had had him since he was a puppy.

Ryder stared at her, one hand on the door, the other on the wheel of his chair. He ran a hand through his hair, leaving it sticking up at the ends. "Anya." His voice was thick and rough with sleep; he wore basketball shorts and a faded Duke University T-shirt that stretched across his lean, muscular chest.

Anya's heart sank. She'd wakened him from sleep in the middle of the night. Another mistake to add to her growing portfolio.

She didn't know what to say, so she began with, "Can I come in?"

"Um, yeah." He moved back and gestured her inside. "Stanley. Back up, buddy."

Anya put her hand down to let Stanley sniff it. He did and then stepped aside, though his expression said he was keeping a sharp eye on her.

Ryder's house had hardwood floors she could see were beautiful, even in the yellow light cast by the small lamp. He shut the front door and moved in front of her to the living room, snapping on another light.

It was furnished tastefully, with a darkly colored sofa against one wall, a leather armchair, a large, low wooden crate for a coffee table and a flat screen TV mounted on a wall painted sage green. The TV was flanked by two tall, and very full, black bookshelves. An orange basketball rested in the corner of the armchair. Books and papers were scattered across both the chair and the crate, along with an open box of Cocoa Krispies.

"You still eat Cocoa Krispies," Anya said, her voice soft.

"Yeah." Looking embarrassed, he rolled to the box and closed its lid, setting it back down on the crate. "Wasn't expecting company."

"I wasn't expecting to *be* company." She motioned toward the sofa. "Okay if I sit?"

"Go ahead."

Somewhere in the room, a clock ticked off the time. Stanley blew out a noisy dog breath and lay on the floor next to Ryder's chair, his tail thumping against the hardwood. Anya stared at her hands, folded in front of her, acutely aware that Ryder's gaze was fixed on her. That he was waiting for her to explain herself.

Easier said than done.

"I talked to Caitlin. Just now. Before I came over here." She still couldn't look at him.

He didn't respond. Wasn't going to make this easy for her.

"She said you know about Annie."

CHAPTER SEVENTEEN

"I thought I knew about Annie," Ryder said. "Turns out I was wrong. The Annie I *thought* I knew doesn't exist."

Anya braved a look at him. "I'm sorry, okay? Just—Sorry."

He shook his head. "I can't figure out why you did it. Pretended to be someone else."

"You wouldn't talk to me. And I…missed you. A lot." The catch in her throat nearly swallowed the words. "I haven't been the same since we broke up. Haven't been myself. Haven't been happy." It was true, she realized. Before the do-over or after it. Same result.

"Ten years is a long time to be unhappy."

"Ten years, three months and—Yes. A long time." She looked at her hands again, clasped so tightly, she could see the whites of her knuckles. "I *thought* I was happy, that I was fine. I worked really hard to make everyone else think so, too."

Now that she thought about it, it had been emotionally draining. Sometimes it had felt as though she took a mask off at night and stored it on her dresser, ready to wear again in the morning. "But the only times I felt good, really good about myself, are the times I was being Annie. And could talk with you. I didn't have to watch what I said. I could be more myself when I was being someone else." She tried a laugh. "Not sure what that says about me. My luck, it's multiple personality disorder."

His gaze was steady, questioning.

"But even then," she bit her lip and shook her head, "I knew it wasn't real. That it had to end. Eventually."

"It couldn't go on forever," he agreed.

"When did you realize it was me?"

"About a month ago, I started to feel as though I'd known you for a long time. Then I slowly realized why that might be. I've only known one person who loved dogs, caramels, and hot springs. Hated sushi and the sound a vacuum cleaner makes. And was irrationally afraid of car washes."

"It's not irrational," she protested. "You put your car in neutral and surrender all control. Those huge brushes. What if they break the windshield? What if there's an earthquake and everything stops but the pink foam? How do you get out of that alive?" Even she knew how silly that sounded, but she wasn't about to admit it.

"Like I said. Not many people."

"I should have been more careful. Made sure she was very different from me. I thought I did, but I guess not."

"If you'd made her that different, I wouldn't have felt—the way I did."

"Did?" *Past tense*. A dull ache of foreboding began in her heart.

"Anya. Look at me."

She did. So did Stanley.

"I know I"—he looked up at the ceiling—"shut you out when you came to see me in rehab. I wasn't ready." His gaze dropped to meet hers. "I didn't know what to do. No future that I could see. Not for me, not for us. I didn't know how to go forward and I sure as hell didn't want to go back."

"I understand," she whispered.

He dropped his gaze to meet hers. "I don't know that you do. You were closer to me than anyone else. What I saw in your eyes. I was—" He sucked in a breath. "I couldn't handle it if that same fear was in mine, too. I didn't want to know. Didn't want to face it. Not then."

"The whole thing was my fault. I turned right in front of a car. It was so stupid. So *stupid*." She looked down at her hands, clenching them into fists, tears welling. "I did that to you. I was the reason you were there."

"I did it to myself. I was the one who got so drunk, you had to drive. And you were furious because I let that girl crawl all over me. You had every right to be mad. Shit, I don't even remember her name or what she looked like."

"Amanda."

"Really?" He sounded surprised. "You remember her name?"

"I hated her. On sight."

"Oh."

Stanley laid his head back down with a sigh. A minute dragged into two, then three. Anya watched resignation settle into Ryder's expression.

"It's late," he said. "It's good we had this…talk. But you should go now. Don't worry about the Annie thing. No big deal. We can forget it happened." He pushed back in his chair.

No. They were finally talking about the accident, getting somewhere. Desperation pushed at her. She couldn't leave. Not now. "You're wrong. It's a great big deal. Could even be illegal."

"Don't worry. I won't press charges."

"And I'm not leaving yet."

His eyes narrowed. "I said, we can forget about it. It's all right. I get it."

"You don't. You don't get it. At all."

Ryder scrubbed his hand over his face. "Then what am I missing? Because it's three a.m. and I'm not thinking straight. We can be"—he exhaled—"friends. Whatever. That's fine. Friends who talk. Sometimes. Can I go back to sleep now?"

"No. You can't and we can't." Anya rose from the sofa and walked to him. At Ryder's side, Stanley rumbled with a low growl.

Ryder wouldn't look at her. He was looking everywhere *but* at her. "I don't want to do this."

"Neither do I. Not really. But if we don't do it now, we never will."

He opened and closed his mouth, finally saying, "I'm good with never."

"I don't think you are. And I'm definitely not."

"Go home, Anya."

She knelt, welcoming the pain of her knees pressing into the hardwood if it could distract her from her twisting insides. She was at eye level with him now and she reached over to lay her hands on his legs. "I never told you I'm sorry. I am. I'm so sorry for that night. For everything that happened."

He squeezed his eyes shut tight, then opened them again. "I'm sorry, too. It never should have happened."

"But it did."

"Not breaking news, Anya. Can we leave it now?"

"No. Say it. The reason you were angry in rehab. The reason you're angry now."

He averted his gaze. "I'm not angry. And I wasn't then." His jaw clenched and a vein pulsed in his neck.

"I don't believe you."

"What the fuck am I supposed to do about that? Believe it."

"No." She shook her head. "I don't."

"Leave," he said again, rougher this time. Louder.

"I'm not leaving until you say. *It.*"

Stanley the dog raised himself to a sitting position, his gaze shifting from Anya to his master, watching them both warily.

"This is bullshit." Ryder's words shot like arrows through the air, straight at her. "You can live in the past all you want, but I'm not going backward. I've worked too hard for that."

"None of that will matter if you don't deal with how you really feel, with what happened. Get it out."

"What are you, a psychologist now?"

"No. Just someone who was there. Who cares about you. Who—" She stopped short of saying she loved him. "I should have come back to see you in rehab. But I didn't. I couldn't."

He leaned forward. "I don't want things to end this way between us. I moved on. You need to," he urged.

End between us. She yanked that arrow out of her heart and threw it aside, ignoring the hole it left. "I can't. Not until we talk about this. *Really* talk about it."

Ryder expelled a breath and sat back hard against the backrest. "Fuck it. I don't need this."

"Well, *I* do. And so do you. Trust me."

"Trust you? *Trust Annie?*"

She flinched. He was right, but she had to stand her ground.

He started to move back again, but this time, she caught the rims of the wheels and held on, preventing him from moving.

"What the hell do you think you're doing?"

"Ryder." She reached up to put her hand on his cheek. The feel of his skin and rough whiskers sent electricity surging through her. "Please."

Her touch changed something in him. His breath caught and then came fast, in sharp spurts. "Don't pity me."

She recoiled at the idea, letting her hand drop to his leg. "I'm feeling a lot of things right now, but believe me, pity isn't one of them."

"I can see it."

"Then you need to get your eyes checked."

He closed his eyes for a long second. She watched him give up on the attempt at deflection.

"Talk to me."

"What do you want me to say, Anya?" His voice was ragged. "That you took away everything I'd worked all my life for when you didn't see that fucking car? That I could have had one hell of a career in the NBA, all my coaches said so, but instead, I ended up in a hospital bed without the use of my legs?"

Anya bit her bottom lip so hard she could taste the blood, warm and accusing. "Yes." Her voice quivered, but she fought to make the words stick. She wasn't giving him any outs.

"Then I'm saying it. But that's not what pisses me off."

"What pisses you off?" Her voice rose, along with his.

"I'm not going there. What's done is done."

"And I'm the one who did it."

"*I'm* the one who was too wasted to drive. I was celebrating. Big game. *Big basketball star.*" Anger spiraled through his voice, emphasizing every word.

"You had a reason to celebrate."

"Dammit, Anya." The emotion in his voice caused it to become throaty, raw. "I told you. It was as much my fault as it was yours."

"I was driving under the influence."

He gaped at her. "You didn't have anything to drink."

"I was so jealous, I couldn't see straight. Might as well have been a red screen in front of my face."

"But that girl. I liked the attention. You were right, I did." His eyes bored into her, watching her reaction. "Yeah, I was feeling it. Practicing for the big time."

She kept her expression passive, didn't let him see how much it hurt. "So you're a normal guy. You like attention from women."

He jerked his hand through his hair. "I'm not doing the my-fault-versus-your-fault thing. I told you, I don't look back."

"Then why won't you let me in? It's because of what you see when you look at me, isn't it? You see that night."

He shook his head, averting his gaze. "No."

"That night I crashed your car. Crashed us."

"No."

"I remind you. Of what you lost."

He refused to look at her. His voice reached a dangerous rumble. "What I *lost* doesn't matter any more."

Anya stood and, in a flash, grabbed the basketball from the chair. "I stole this from you. *This*. The game you loved, that you were so talented at, you could have played pro." To her ears, her voice sounded unnaturally high, on the verge of breaking.

She threw the ball to him. His hands went up automatically, deftly catching it, the basketball making its familiar metallic ping when it hit his grasp. He looked at her, looked at the ball, and back at her again. Then he threw it, hard, against the bookcase to her right. The bookcase made a cracking noise and shuddered. Books crashed and fell, along with a small stone piece of art that survived the fall, but made a dent in the floor.

Stanley whimpered. The basketball bounced backward and made a long, slow roll toward Ryder.

He fastened his gaze on the ball and picked it up when it reached him. He examined it and then, holding it with one hand, lowered it to the floor beside him. He released it. "That's not what I lost," he said quietly.

She crossed the room to crouch before him. This time, she was the one who couldn't make eye contact.

He leaned forward and reached out to hold her face in his hands, urging her to look at him. When she did, he said, "I lost you. I couldn't ask you to stay with me. I wasn't who I used to be. That hurt a hell of a lot more."

His warm breath tickled her face as his warm, strong fingers on her skin stirred a deep longing for more of his touch, for his hands stroking her body. "I thought you couldn't love me any more." A hiccup drowned her last word. "Because of what I did."

"We both have guilt we can't let go of."

"I want to," she whispered.

"Then take the ball." He held it out to her.

She hesitated, not sure whether she could do it.

"Take it," he bit out.

She did, then rose and turned. The basketball shivered in her hands. It took her a minute to realize she was the one doing the shivering and the ball was just along for the ride. She closed her eyes and threw it, as hard as she could, at the same spot Ryder had nearly demolished.

A resounding crash. Then another. And another. When she opened her eyes, she saw the bookcase had given up its fight this time, falling in on itself to rest in pieces on the floor. "Oh, shit."

From behind her, Ryder remarked, "I'm going to have to make another trip to Ikea."

She spun to face him, not sure whether to cry or laugh. Her body felt incredibly weary, as though adrenaline had surged through it and made a quiet exit, leaving nothing behind.

She sank to the floor in front of him.

"How did it feel?"

"Good," she admitted.

"Yeah. Good. A basketball is cheaper than therapy."

"Don't joke about this."

He shifted in the chair. "I don't know what else to do."

She saw his heart exposed in his dark eyes. Wanting, hoping. The same things she was certain were in her own eyes. She moved closer to him. Their faces were nearly touching now. His lips were so close to hers, his eyes, his face, pulling her in to his world, one where she'd felt safe, warm, loved. And on fire.

"You don't know what you'd be signing up for." His voice was uneven, bumping along a road without signs.

She put her hand on the back of his neck. "I'd be signing up for you."

Their lips moved closer, so slowly that she thought she might pass out from the anticipation. She wanted him, wanted him so badly. His scent—of soap and sleep and heady with masculinity—enveloped her.

Ryder pulled back from her abruptly, rubbed his face and stared at the mess by the bookcase.

Nooooo. Anya blinked.

"This isn't going to work. You need to go."

Not happening. She straightened her shoulders, feeling as though she were emerging from a fog that kept trying to pull her back into its depths. Disappointment nudged anticipation aside. "I can't drive home. It's too late. I'd never make it."

He pulled his mouth tight. "Then I'll get you a blanket and a pillow. You can sleep on my sofa and leave first thing."

Not the sleeping arrangement she'd been hoping for a minute ago, but she'd have to take it. "Okay," she said. "Thanks."

He pushed back, leaving her crouched on the floor alone. Stanley padded along behind his master, disappearing into the hallway. Anya stood, stretching her aching legs.

Before she could fully process what was happening, Ryder reappeared, holding a blanket and pillow. "Here you go. Bathroom is down the hall that way." He pointed. "There's an extra toothbrush in the cabinet, if you want it." He pointed again. "And the kitchen is that way if you want coffee before you go."

"Ryder—"

He arched his brow in a way that made it clear he didn't want to answer any questions.

"Nothing." He wasn't going to continue what they'd started; that much was clear. She shook her head. "Thanks."

"Good night, Anya."

"Good night, Ryder." God help her, it felt like goodbye.

A few minutes later, she tiptoed into the bathroom. The doorway was larger than she was accustomed to, with a door that opened outward. Inside, the room was large and open, with plenty of room for a wheelchair to move and rails next to the fixtures. The shower, built with a seat inside, was flush with the floor. No threshold.

Once she'd finished, which included borrowing and using a toothbrush still in its package, she tiptoed back out, shut the door without making a sound, and made her way back to the sofa in the living room. She laid down, her head on the pillow and the blanket tucked in around her. She sniffed the pillow, hoping the case would carry his scent, but it was only the generic scent of fresh linen.

She was bone-tired and ready for sleep, but her body refused to let her forget that Ryder slept only a couple of rooms away. Images floated before her mind's eye. Memories. All those times they'd made love at the hot springs, before the accident. When they kissed at the photo shoot only a few days ago.

That fast, she leapt ahead to a new image. Her and Ryder in his bedroom, making love with a fierceness neither had known before.

She glanced over her shoulder at the ruins of the bookcase, looming over her in the dark. This wasn't going to be easy.

CHAPTER EIGHTEEN

Anya dozed off at some point, waking as the first light of morning peeked through the living room blinds. It didn't take her any time to orient; she'd not forgotten for one second that she was in Ryder's house.

He wasn't up, yet. She would have heard him. Maybe she could offer to make and bring him coffee. Yes, a nice thing to do and only polite of a houseguest. That's the only reason she was thinking of going into his room. It wasn't as though she were hoping he was naked and willing to welcome her into his arms.

No, it wasn't like that at all.

Careful not to make a sound, she sat up, grabbed her bag, and reached for a brush. Once satisfied she'd done the best she could with her sofa hair, she smoothed her top and tiptoed in her bare feet to the hallway leading to his bedroom.

She paused to listen at the door. Still no sound. She knocked, very quietly, and heard him say, "Come in." He sounded wide-awake.

Closing a trembling hand around the knob, she turned it and opened the door. From the platform bed in the center of the room, Ryder watched her without saying a word.

Her stomach did a flip. He hadn't been able to sleep, either.

"I—wondered if I could make you a cup of coffee."

"I don't want coffee." He gestured her forward, the muscles in his bare chest rippling. "Come here."

He meant—oh God, he did. It was an invitation. In her relief, in her eagerness, she plunged forward, but at the last minute, tried to pull back because she thought maybe she shouldn't be so impatient. The start/stop twisted her feet and she fell into a face-first sprawl on his bed.

She raised her head to see him shaking his head and clicking his tongue against the roof of his mouth. "Alice...Alice," he said with a sigh, "*One* of us has to be able to stand upright."

She smiled at the use of the Zest photographer's name for her and received a reluctant grin in return.

Ryder's expression softened. "Come here," he said again.

The hell with patience. She scrambled up the length of the bed on her hands and knees until she reached his arms, which immediately wrapped around her. His skin was warm against hers, his touch achingly familiar. She'd missed it, missed him, so much.

He kissed her forehead, gently, slowly.

"Ryder."

"Don't talk."

She could only honor that request for a few minutes. Then the words rushed out, tripping over each other. "Last night you could barely speak to me. You didn't even want me on your sofa. Now we're in your bed. You're kissing me."

His chest moved against her as he took a deep breath and then wrapped her tighter in his embrace. "Am I? Hadn't noticed."

She looked up at him, imploring him with her eyes. "Be serious. What changed? I have to know." She waited for his response. And waited longer.

Finally, he put one arm up, his hand behind his head, and held her close with his other arm. "Yeah, that's kept me up all night."

She didn't speak, waiting for him to continue.

"I just didn't know. How I felt."

She put her hand on his chest, her fingers splayed, as if she could somehow keep the hurt from his heart. "Angry. I know. You have a right to—"

"Not that at all."

She looked up at him. "Explain it to me."

"My life is good. Pretty amazing, really. I love my job, love working with my team. I had to think about things for a while." He paused. "As in, all the rest of the night. Not that there was a lot of it left."

From a dog bed nearby, Anya heard Stanley sigh, then get up and move into the other room, his toenails clicking on the floor.

"Oh yeah," Ryder called after him. "I have a great dog, too."

Anya tried to smile, but couldn't quite manage it. He'd said his life was good. Amazing. He didn't need her in it.

"I don't know that I would have made it to the NBA. Or that I would have been able to last as a pro. It might have sucked."

"Money, fame. Sure." Her mind was only half on that. She was wondering how she was going to climb out of this bed without letting her devastation show. He didn't need her in his life. *Hold on.*

She'd told him to explain it to her and he was trying. She had to pay attention, no matter how much it hurt.

"What I didn't realize is how I really felt. About you."

Great. Now was when she decided to pay attention. Anya screwed her eyes shut tight, waiting. *Here it comes. He can't be with me because of what I did. What he did. Whether he would have wanted that pro career or not.*

He lowered his arm and turned on his side by shifting his upper body. He put a hand under her chin, lifting it so her eyes met his. "I tell my guys, never give up on the play. Persevere."

"The play."

"I didn't give it a chance to work. Didn't give *us* a chance. Once everything happened, I decided you were better off without me."

"I am never better off without you," she said fervently. "Clearly." Despite her best intentions, hope lifted inside her.

"I want to be with you, Anya," he said, his voice rumbling straight through her. "You're my swish."

Um—what? Hope got stuck between floors. Did he mean sweetie…ish?

Her confusion must have shown on her face because he rushed to say, "Swish. The perfect sound, the perfect feeling. The ball dropping through the basket." He shook his head. "I'll lose the basketball metaphors. That was the last one, I promise."

A slow smile spread across her face. She felt herself relax in his arms. He wanted to be with her. He could use all the basketball metaphors he wanted to. The perfect feeling. *Swish.*

"How about this, instead?" he said. "I can't promise this is going to be easy, but I can promise I'll do my best." He leaned toward her, his mouth nearly closing in on hers.

"I can't promise I'll stay upright, but I'll try," she whispered. "Not now, though."

"You think?" He kissed her, long and deeply, pulling her closer still. Her breasts were against his chest, her nipples signaling their extreme pleasure at this turn of events.

He pulled back, watching her. He kissed her on the forehead again, just above her nose and then tucked a piece of hair behind her ear. "Let's talk about you. Are you going to be able to leave the accident behind us, or if we're together, am I going to be a constant reminder?"

She pondered that. "I think it will always be with me, in some ways, but now I want it to be because I learned not to put myself in that situation again, where I lose control, make a bad decision that affects someone else."

"Everybody makes mistakes. And I think the ones you and I made that night cancel each other out."

Stark honesty shone in his eyes. He'd never looked more endearingly vulnerable, yet strong, to her. She nodded. "I can leave it behind."

"Me, too."

"Start fresh."

"Fresh," he repeated. "But there's something else."

She raised her brows in a question.

"You said you were unhappy. That's not all about me."

The scar she'd once borne, and the misery she had associated with it, flashed before her eyes. She lowered her gaze, fixing it on his chest. "I'm afraid of sounding like I'm whining or like I don't appreciate what I have."

"Hey, it's me." He touched her nose lightly with his finger. "You used to tell me everything."

"Everything." She nodded.

"Tell me what's going on with you."

First, she had to know herself. She thought. Thought hard. At last she said, "I don't want what I do in life to be so focused on what I look like." Once the words were out, she felt a surge of relief. "I don't want to be a photo, a face and a body that could be anyone."

"I like your face and body."

"Photos get doctored, made to look better than me. Half the time, I don't even recognize myself. Or worse, I start thinking my skin really does look that good."

"It's pretty great."

"Focus," she told him.

"Okay." He crossed his heart. "Focusing. Not that it's easy when we're talking about your body, which is, let's face it, right here next to me."

Hard not to take that as a compliment, but she badly wanted him to get what she was saying. "Relying on what you look like in a photo is subjective, superficial, and—and—and—"

"Scary?" he offered.

"Scary. Yes." She nodded. "It's not what really counts, what lasts."

"I can understand that. You want more. You want people to see more in you. But your job at Zest isn't only modeling, is it?"

"No, but the part that isn't is focused on what *other* people look like. So..."

"So it doesn't make you happy."

"I want to leave." As soon as she said it out loud, she knew it was right.

"Then leave. Go in a different direction. What would you like to do?"

She hesitated. "I haven't fully thought it out."

"Then try it out on me."

She dropped her voice, feeling suddenly shy. "I'd like to open a place for dogs. Day care, boarding, grooming, a store. I've saved some money and I inherited some from my grandfather. I think I could do it."

A slow grin spread across his face. "I know you could do it. That's a great idea. You love dogs. They love you. And they see hearts, not faces."

She answered his grin with one of her own. "Exactly."

"Just *for* the record, though."

"Yes?"

"I think you're as beautiful on the inside as you are on the outside. You're brave, kind—"

"So a Girl Scout, basically." She wasn't sure how she felt about that.

"I remember a side of you that was a lot more adventurous than any Girl Scout would be. So would you be quiet for a minute and let me finish? I don't say these kinds of things a lot. I'm a guy."

"Please. Go on." She couldn't stop the giggle.

His voice became husky. "You make me laugh, you make me think, you make me happy, you make me mad. Most of all, you make me *feel*. For a while, I was afraid I didn't have that any more."

Butterflies flapped their wings furiously inside her, while bells pealed and fireworks whistled through the air. Ryder, her Ryder. "I love you," she said. And then froze. What if he didn't say it back? What if he wasn't ready for that part, yet?

"I love you, too. Anya. Annie. *Whoever* you are."

"Anya," she said solemnly, holding out her hand. "Nice to meet you."

"Nice to meet you, too." His mouth closed in on hers and his chest pressed into hers. She could feel his erection through the basketball shorts he wore.

"Anything else I make you?" she asked when they came up for air.

"Oh hell," was his answer as he began tugging at her top. Once he'd pulled it over her shoulders and dispensed with her bra, which flew across the room to land somewhere around Stanley's dog bed, he cupped her breasts with his hand and began teasing her nipples with his tongue.

"I've missed you. So much," she whispered.

Next to go were her jeans and thong. Where they flew to, she didn't know or care.

She pulled at his shorts and tugged them all the way down and off his legs. She tossed them without looking at where they landed. They'd be found eventually. Then she took him in her hands, reveling in the feel of his swollen penis and the memory of what it could do to her. *With* her.

"You first," he groaned. "Turn. Please." He gestured for her to switch positions, so that her head was by the end of the bed. He took her then, his tongue exploring the most sensitive parts of her, then teasing out an orgasm that had her clutching the bed sheets and filling the room with her cries of blissful agony.

Once it had shuddered through her in waves, she looked back up at him to see a wicked grin on his face. "Want to be on top?"

"I would *love* to be on top," she said, running her fingers up his body until they cupped his balls and stroked his penis, softly, teasingly, and then more urgently. When his dick was rocklike in its stiffness, she straddled his hips and steered him inside her, where his penis plunged hard and deep. She lifted up and down in an easy rhythm as he cupped and massaged her breasts, her nipples standing at attention.

They came together, in one breathtaking explosion that left them spent and out of breath. Anya raked her hair out of her eyes and collapsed at his side, damp and exhilarated. Ryder found her hand and they lay on their backs on the bed, staring up at the ceiling.

"Wow," said Ryder.

"Wow," agreed Anya.

"Tell me why, again, we haven't been doing this for the last ten years."

"We had some things to work out."

"We're good now, right?"

She propped herself up on one elbow to look into his dark eyes and melt, one more time. "We're so good." She sucked in a breath. "When will you be ready to go again?"

He laughed. And reached for her.

CHAPTER NINETEEN

Fourteen months later

The late September day was a gorgeous one to be in the forest, surrounded by tall, lush trees with leaves in bright bold colors. As much as the setting was a feast for the eyes, the smell—of fresh, clean air tinged with earth—was intoxicating. Anya breathed in deep, her lungs deprived of this for far too long.

At her side on the trail, Ryder rolled slowly to a stop in a spot where sunlight streamed through the trees to puddle on the packed dirt. He tipped his chin back, letting his face bathe in the warm glow. "Man, that feels good."

The two of them hadn't been on this trail in more than eleven years now. Anya had looked it up online out of curiosity and been surprised to learn it had been made wheelchair accessible. Ryder had done a lot of things Anya wouldn't have thought possible—including kayaking and playing table tennis—but he hadn't tried hiking a trail before today.

It wasn't easy, but it was doable for a person with his arm strength. The trail had been flattened in places, which made it easier for him to navigate it. Their secret hot springs spot was tucked away off the trail, but not too far. They didn't know how easy or difficult it would be for Ryder to traverse the side trail, but were willing to at least attempt it.

Anya stooped down to sniff a wildflower. "Beautiful," she said. "I'm glad we're here. I'm going to sketch it when we get back." She'd started sketching again not long ago, when she had time between everything she had to do to get her new dog spa and boarding facility open. It was more involved and more worth it than she could have ever imagined. Ryder liked to say that she practically floated with happiness right now.

"I'm glad we're here, too." Ryder reached out to squeeze her hand and then began rolling again.

She hastened to keep up with him. Wasn't easy. He was so strong; he could beat her in a race most of the time. She loved watching him play basketball, rolling up and down the court with even more intensity and speed than he'd had as a college player. For his birthday, she'd done a charcoal sketch of him in an action shot taken from a photo and then framed it. His expression had contained a mixture of pride, determination, and fierce competitiveness.

She loved it.

Her Ryder.

After they'd gone about another half mile, they recognized the turnoff at the exact same moment. "All this time," she marveled, "and we both still know exactly where it is."

"Memories like that don't fade." Ryder winked at her. "But now it's time to make new ones. Let's do this."

Anya pulled her phone from her backpack, just to check that she still had service. If something should happen, she needed to be able to get help. She wasn't going, otherwise. Her cell was only one bar down. Pretty good, considering they were fairly deep into the forest. "You're on," she said.

As they followed the side trail, squirrels scampered up trees, only to stop and blink at them, and birds high on branches heralded their arrival with cries that echoed ahead. The trail became a little rough in parts, particularly when they had to cross over large tree roots, but they managed with Anya giving Ryder a push in spots and him using his arms to shift his weight, ensuring he remained balanced.

Less than an hour later, they arrived at the small clearing with the hot springs.

"Omigod," Anya breathed. "It's just the same."

Ryder turned to her with a wry smile. "We change; nature doesn't. Much."

"I'd forgotten how beautiful a place this is." She shrugged the backpack off and set it down.

"I hadn't," he said quietly.

They were silent for a few minutes, taking it all in and watching the sun stream through the top of the tall trees to glint on water edged by a small cloud of steam.

"Ready?" Anya asked.

"Ready."

They'd worn swimsuits under their clothes, in case the springs were no longer as private as they had once been. It had, after all, been eleven years. Ryder had joked that there could be a strip mall there by now. Anya had just looked at him and drawled, "Speaking of stripping…" Then they'd done just that and fallen into bed laughing.

Anya peeled off her clothes, down to her swimsuit, and watched Ryder do the same. She folded their clothes and put them on top of the backpack.

"No," he said. "I'd like to keep my pants over here." He gestured toward a rock to his left on the edge of the springs.

Anya looked at him, puzzled. "Won't they get wet?"

"They'll be fine."

She shrugged and handed him his pants. "Okay."

He leaned down and put them next to the pool. Then he locked the chair and moved the footrests aside. She helped him out of the chair, something he could usually do himself, but in this situation, it was harder than normal.

"Ooof," she said. It was a good thing she'd started working out as much as he did. She now had actual muscle tone in her arms.

She joined Ryder in sitting on the edge of the springs, on the smooth rocks. After looking around, she said, "We haven't seen any people for a couple of hours." Her voice lifted hopefully.

"Thought you'd never ask." He grinned, lowered himself into the shallow pool, and pulled off his swim trunks. Then he circled them overhead and tossed them to the side. "Your turn."

He watched, whistling with appreciation as she unfastened her bikini top and threw it to rest on top of his trunks.

"Sssshhh!" she mock scolded him. "We don't want to attract attention, remember?"

"Oh, right." Ryder made an exaggerated show of being quiet and then wiggled his eyebrows in a clear suggestion when she removed her bikini bottom and also threw it aside.

Anya joined him then, pressing her breasts into his chest and resting her elbows on his broad shoulders. She could feel his erection, stiff and ready in the steaming water. "I can't believe we're here again. After all this time."

"The more things change…" he murmured. His mouth closed on hers, his tongue probing, questioning.

He felt so good, so right. The water bathed them gently, wrapping them in its soothing warmth as they made love, slowly and surely. She abandoned the need for quiet as she came in an explosion of fire from within, and the forest creatures heard her cry out and then whisper Ryder's name over and over.

At last, they sat back against the stones worn smooth by time. Anya was sure she'd never been so fully and completely sated. Ryder the man was an even more giving lover than he'd been as a college sophomore. She tried her best to match him in that and the result was something nearly magical.

She closed her eyes. "We should come next year, too."

There was a vague rustling next to her. Ryder repositioning himself, she supposed. Then he spoke. "And the year after that, and the one after that. I hope we're still coming here when we're sixty."

Anya smiled, opened her eyes, and turned to him. Before she could answer, she saw what he held in his hand. A small box. "What's that?"

He opened it. A diamond ring glittered in a small shaft of sunlight that had come through the trees.

"Omigod," she breathed. "Ryder."

"Will you marry me? I'd get down on one knee, but—let's just say that's not happening."

The ring was perfect. A solitaire, princess cut, set in white gold. The only kind of engagement ring she'd ever thought she'd want, the few times she'd thought about it. Though she'd never told Ryder that. Or anyone else. "Yes," she said, her eyes brimming. "*Yes.* I can't think of anything I'd rather do."

"Good. Because if you didn't want it, I was going to have to find a bear to give it to." His eyes crinkled at the corners as he grinned.

She hugged him, her heart full, and kissed him long and hard. "Where are we going to tell our children you proposed? We have to get our stories straight."

"Already we have to? For these kids we don't have yet?" He laughed. "So we tell them it was right here. But in our story, we're clothed."

"Perfect. But we don't have to rush into making that true quite yet, do we?"

"Are you going to be like this when we're sixty?"

"Worse," she vowed. "So baby, get used to it."

ABOUT THE AUTHOR

Jane Lynne Daniels grew up a city girl, only to meet the love of her life at the annual Volunteer Fireman's Ball in tiny Grass Valley, Oregon. She and her husband and dogs recently moved from the Pacific Northwest to Ohio, where they miss the rain and ocean but love the change in seasons. Jane is doing her best to adopt a Midwest accent, but since people look at her funny when she tries, it probably isn't working.

She is also the author of *Be Careful What You Kiss For* and *Kiss Happens* in the Love Rewritten series, and the two short stories, *Grab the Brass Ring* and *Say It Again, Sam.*

Did you enjoy this book? Drop us a line and say so! We love to hear from readers, and so do our authors. To connect, visit www.boroughspublishinggroup.com online, send comments directly to info@boroughspublishinggroup.com, or friend us on Facebook and Twitter. And be sure to check back regularly for contests and new releases in your favorite subgenres of romance!

Are you an aspiring writer? Check out www.boroughspublishinggroup.com/submit and see if we can help you make your dreams come true.

www.ingramcontent.com/pod-product-compliance
Lightning Source LLC
Chambersburg PA
CBHW071626140626

46555CB00021B/499